THE R
OF
BARBARA CARTLAND

Barbaracartland.com Ltd

.com

POD Preparation by M-Y Books
m-ybooks.co.uk

THE BARBARA CARTLAND PINK COLLECTION

Barbara Cartland was the most prolific bestselling author in the history of the world. She was frequently in the Guinness Book of Records for writing more books in a year than any other living author. In fact her most amazing literary feat was when her publishers asked for more Barbara Cartland romances, she doubled her output from 10 books a year to over 20 books a year, when she was 77.

She went on writing continuously at this rate for 20 years and wrote her last book at the age of 97, thus completing 400 books between the ages of 77 and 97.

Her publishers finally could not keep up with this phenomenal output, so at her death she left 160 unpublished manuscripts, something again that no other author has ever achieved.

Now the exciting news is that these 160 original unpublished Barbara Cartland books are ready for publication and they will be published by Barbaracartland.com exclusively on the internet, as the web is the best possible way to reach so many Barbara Cartland readers around the world.

The 160 books will be published monthly and will be numbered in sequence.

The series is called the Pink Collection as a tribute to Barbara Cartland whose favourite colour was pink and it became very much her trademark over the years.

The Barbara Cartland Pink Collection is published only on the internet. Log on to www.barbaracartland.com to find out how you can purchase the books monthly as they are published, and take out a subscription that will ensure that all subsequent editions are delivered to you by mail order to your home.

TITLES IN THIS SERIES

THE LATE DAME BARBARA CARTLAND

Barbara Cartland, who sadly died in May 2000 at the grand age of ninety eight, remains one of the world's most famous romantic novelists. With worldwide sales of over one billion, her outstanding 723 books have been translated into thirty six different languages, to be enjoyed by readers of romance globally.

Writing her first book "Jigsaw" at the age of 21, Barbara became an immediate bestseller. Building upon this initial success, she wrote continuously throughout her life, producing bestsellers for an astonishing 76 years. In addition to Barbara Cartland's legion of fans in the UK and across Europe, her books have always been immensely popular in the USA. In 1976 she achieved the unprecedented feat of having books at numbers 1 & 2 in the prestigious B. Dalton Bookseller bestsellers list.

Although she is often referred to as the "Queen of Romance", Barbara Cartland also wrote several historical biographies, six autobiographies and numerous theatrical plays as well as books on life, love, health and cookery. Becoming one of Britain's most popular media personalities and dressed in her trademark pink, Barbara spoke on radio and television about social and political issues, as well as making many public appearances.

In 1991 she became a Dame of the Order of the British Empire for her contribution to literature and her work for humanitarian and charitable causes.

Known for her glamour, style, and vitality Barbara Cartland became a legend in her own lifetime. Best remembered for her wonderful romantic novels and loved by millions of readers worldwide, her books remain treasured for their heroic heroes, plucky heroines and traditional values. But above all, it was Barbara Cartland's overriding belief in the positive power of love to help, heal and improve the quality of life for everyone that made her truly unique.

"Love is certainly a many splendoured thing, but it is wealth of other things as well."

Barbara Cartland

CHAPTER 1
1899

Moira Strathcarron lopped the top off her egg and sighed.

Although outside the windows of Lednock Castle it was a fine sunny day, the feeling around the breakfast table was far from congenial.

Her family had been at Lednock Castle for over three hundred years and never had things been so bad as they were now. A succession of disastrous harvests, coupled with her father having made some ill-advised investments that had substantially drained the family coffers over the past twenty years.

Although beautiful and situated in one of the most picturesque parts of Scotland, deep in the heart of the Trossach Mountains overlooking Loch Earn, the estate was fast becoming a huge financial burden.

So on this bright June morning something the Earl did not need was news that his family were about to endure the ordeal and expense of visitors.

Moira held her breath as her mother finished reading out the letter that had just arrived.

"I am sorry, Margaret, we cannot entertain the notion of a visitor," said the Earl.

"But this Larry Harwood is a great friend of Lord and Lady Cunningham in London. We cannot refuse him, it would cause great offence."

1

The Countess was quite adamant. The reputation of the family was at stake and she had no wish to compromise it.

"I fail to see why they should take offence," said Ewen, the Earl's only son, as he helped himself to a bowl of porridge. "It is not as if we owe this Larry Harwood anything he is no kin of ours."

"Whisht, brother Ewen," whispered Moira. "The Cunninghams are great friends of ours. Did you not say when they visited us last spring that you found them amusing company?"

Ewen took his bowl of porridge and sat down next to his sister.

He was a fine-looking young man with the same fiery red hair as his mother. He cared deeply about his lineage and the castle. In fact he had ignored his father's wish that he join the Army in favour of a more rustic life overseeing the tenant farms on the estate.

He was never happier than when he was herding the sheep or taking care of the prize bullocks that Lednock was justly famous for.

"Mother, perhaps this American fellow would bring others to Lednock Castle," suggested Moira. "I have heard that it is becoming quite fashionable to have paying guests in some parts of the Highlands – "

She tailed off as she saw the look on her father's face.

"I will not stoop to paying guests," he fumed, banging his spoon down on the table. Almost immediately, seeing that he had upset his daughter whom he loved enormously, the Earl softened a little.

"But perhaps we can make some money out of him by taking him on shoots. Aye, I will speak to MacGregor, the gamekeeper, to see how our stocks of grouse are fairing."

After breakfast Moira went to her mother who was busy inspecting the blue room in the West wing.

"Mother – " she began.

The Countess turned round with a strained smile.

"You must not mind your father's ill humour, he has so much to worry about at present," she said, tenderly smoothing down a lock of Moira's dark hair. "It is vital that this year's harvest will be a good one and that the estate will start to make money again."

"Are matters really so bad, mother?" Moira looked at her pleadingly.

"I am afraid they are, my darling. And yes, we may have to postpone our plans to visit Edinburgh."

"I am sure that I can find diversions here at Lednock," replied Moira bravely. "And if Mr. Harwood is to be our guest, then I can take him out riding along the brae."

The Countess smiled gratefully at her daughter – she was so proud of her.

Although she had not inherited her own red hair and green eyes, she was the image of her father – the dark eyes, the noble brow and the thick mass of dark brown hair.

She was barely eighteen, but the Countess could see that Moira was becoming a beauty in her own special way.

"That would be lovely, dearest. Now, I must see that this room is fit to receive our guest. I think your father is coming round to the idea and we should make ready."

Over the next week, the castle was cleaned from top to bottom by a group of women who lived locally. The

3

Countess had retained only a small staff at Lednock and having such an important visitor meant she needed more help. She was mindful of making a good impression on their American guest.

Moira helped her father send out invitations for a weekend shooting party. She addressed the envelopes to a whole host of local worthies, many of whom they had not entertained for quite some time.

*

Then the day eventually dawned when the mysterious Larry Harwood was due to arrive. The castle was in a frenzy of activity so Moira and Ewen went on a long walk to avoid the bustle.

"I wonder what this American fellow will be like?" mused Moira with just the tiniest hint of romantic interest, "do you think he will be young and handsome?"

"Probably old and fat, if he is a friend of the Cunninghams!" replied Ewen, sarcastically.

"I have never met an American before," continued Moira as they strode amongst the heather, "they say that they can be a trifle loud and boastful."

"And they say that all Scots are mean and dour," answered Ewen with a smile. "So we will show him that's not true either, won't we?"

"Ewen, do you really think that the estate is in terrible trouble?"

He took his sister's hand and squeezed it, gently.

"I ken that a good harvest would change our fortunes so that is what we must pray for. Come now, sister, I will race you to the top of the brae."

Larry Harwood arrived that Friday after breakfast and everyone except the Earl came out to greet him. It had been a long time since the castle had seen so much luggage or commotion.

"Welcome to Lednock Castle," called the Countess, walking out to greet their visitor. "I do hope you will enjoy your stay with us."

Harwood was short, corpulent and in his late thirties. His clothes were very different from anything the family had ever seen and he wore a large hat on top of slicked-down brown hair.

The Countess noted that his choice of tie was a trifle garish for the country and that his boots would not stand him in good stead should he wish to go for walks.

Upon seeing him for the first time, Moira shuddered to think that she had entertained any notions that he might provide a romantic diversion.

"Your Ladyship," he cried, grasping the Countess's hand so firmly that she thought that her bones would break. His beady blue eyes were watery and disappeared into creases of fat when he smiled.

"Thank you so much for inviting me into your home. I've never stayed in a real-live castle before. We don't have them back in the States."

He paused for a moment as he viewed the magnificent turrets and structure of Lednock Castle.

"Say, how old do you say the place is?"

"It was built in 1520 and then Mary, Queen of Scots gave it to the first Earl of Strathcarron in 1542," answered the Countess.

"A real Queen?" he gulped, his fleshy mouth hanging open. "Land snake's alive! I take off my hat."

Moira nudged Ewen, barely able to stifle a giggle, as Larry's hat remained firmly on his head.

"Rankin, the butler, will show you to your room," suggested the Countess, taken aback by her guest's brash manner.

"He shouts as if he is on top of a mountain," whispered Moira to her brother, as the American commented loudly upon everything he encountered.

"Perhaps he is deaf?" offered Ewen mischievously.

Just then, the Countess appeared and shooed them away from the foot of the staircase.

"Mr. Harwood will want some refreshment after he has unpacked. Moira, would you please go and tell cook that we will take tea in the drawing room in ten minutes?"

Moira nodded and headed for the kitchens, where she was stunned to see that the table was laden with delicacies that had not been seen at Lednock in many years.

"Tea in ten minutes, please, cook."

She took a step forward as she noticed a dish of the black shiny eggs on the table. "Caviar!" she exclaimed. "I have not eaten caviar for ages."

"That has got to last us, my Lady. So please ask that brother of yours to go easy with his spoon."

Cook was shaking her head as the footman brought in a hamper that clearly bore the Fortnum and Mason's crest. Moira's eyes were wide with delight but she could not help feeling nervous too she knew there was no money for this kind of extravagance.

From the moment that Larry Harwood set foot inside the Castle, he did indeed make himself at home.

The family was served porridge for breakfast, whilst Larry had a hot buffet to choose from. They nibbled on dark bread and collops made from minced leftovers, but Larry had his pick of the contents of the Fortnum's hamper.

"He doesn't seem to notice that we are not eating the same food as him," protested Moira. "We are forced to eat servant's food while he eats us out of house and home. And what an appetite he has. Do you know he ate no less than four chops at dinner last night?"

"Aye," agreed Ewen grimly. "I had to order one of our prize sheep to be slaughtered for it. We were keeping it for Christmas too."

"Then there is this shooting party at the weekend. I dread to think what we might be forced to eat with so many guests probably leftovers. How long is he here for?"

"Three weeks, I believe father said."

"And then there is the nonsense he talks. Did you hear that ridiculous story over breakfast about picking gold nuggets the size of a hen's egg out of the rivers in California? I do not believe him for one moment."

"But he has money, that much is certain," said Ewen. "He sports a diamond-topped walking cane – though it will be not much use in the mountains."

The pair started to laugh at the thought of Larry in his loud suits and unsuitable boots, trying to negotiate the rocky outcrops of the Trossachs.

But not everyone in the castle shared their thinly veiled contempt of the visitor.

Ewen began to notice how his father would linger long after dinner with the American and then take him into the library for whisky and cigars.

He did not mention this to Moira or his mother, as he did not wish to alarm them, but he felt certain that something was going on behind closed doors that he was not going to like.

He pushed these thoughts aside as all too soon the day of the shooting party dawned. There had been a lot of excitement in the village as MacGregor began to hire men as beaters for the weekend.

The schedule was decided by the Earl – early on Saturday morning the first shooting party would leave the castle and on Sunday, there would be a hunt.

Those who could not be accommodated at the castle would stay with Lord Crieff who lived nearby. He was one of the Earl's oldest friends and even he was taken aback when introduced to their American guest. Innately suspicious of strangers, Lord Crieff had huffed and puffed at Larry's over-friendly manner.

Moira had not been invited to go out on the grouse shoot, so she made herself busy helping her mother. While she was handing out sticks and boots, she noticed a young man standing on his own whom she did not know.

'I wonder who he could be?' she thought wistfully eyeing him. 'He seems so out of place at this gathering.'

The young man was tall and handsome with long flowing hair that reminded her of a cavalier's. He held the air of one who preferred his own company.

He caught her gaze and smiled, bowing his head respectfully.

Moira blushed to the roots of her hair and hurried away.

She desperately wanted to find out who this charming stranger could be, but she knew that if she asked Ewen, he would only make fun of her.

Moira watched as the young man set off with the rest of the party. Was it her imagination or did he look back at her as they turned the corner into the drive?

Her heart leapt and she suddenly felt incredibly light – she could not wait until he returned later that afternoon.

*

The party was out until teatime. Larry returned with several brace of grouse bragging about his prowess. His voice could be heard well before he came into view.

Moira rushed outside and looked hopefully for the young man who had stirred her earlier.

She searched eagerly for him, but to her enormous disappointment, could see no sign of him.

Feeling quite deflated, she circled around the castle intending to visit the vegetable garden. She often came here to be alone as only cook and the gardener ventured into it.

As she turned the corner, she saw a figure standing by the runner beans. At first, she thought it must be the gardener, but as she drew closer, she caught her breath.

'It is he,' she thought to herself.

Sensing someone was close, the young man turned to face her. He seemed quite embarrassed to be caught inspecting the blossoming runner beans and became flustered.

"I beg your pardon," he bowed low, his long hair falling forwards over his collar.

"I had quite tired of the company I was keeping and sought some peace and quiet. I could not help but notice that your runner beans have an unpleasant infestation."

He pointed to the leaves that were covered in black insects.

"I would have a word with your gardener. He must take steps to remedy this blight or you'll have no crop later in the summer."

"Why – thank you," stammered Moira, surprised that such a gentleman should be so interested in horticulture.

"You are a gardener yourself?" she asked him, nervously.

"No, sadly not. But I am forgetting my manners. Stuart Weston at your service."

Moira noticed that his eyes were a startling shade of pale blue. The sun danced on his brown hair, bringing out its reddish highlights – she thought that his hair would not disgrace a woman as it was so lustrous and thick.

"My name is Moira," she said, quietly. "Are you a friend of my father's?"

"I know him a little. Your brother and I have had dealings with each other. It was good to spend some time with them both today."

"And are you staying with us or with Lord Crieff?"

"Oh, nothing so grand for me. I will be staying at the inn this evening."

Moira suddenly felt an overwhelming impulse to invite him to stay at Lednock, but she knew that it would be far too forward of her to do so.

Stuart took a step back and bowed once more.

"Now, if you will excuse me, Moira, I should retire to my lodgings. I have no appetite for the drinking that goes on after these events and wish to be fresh for the hunt tomorrow. Will I have the pleasure of seeing you then?"

'He is so handsome,' Moira thought, as she nodded her assent. 'I must find out some more about this very intriguing gentleman.'

*

It was with some surprise that the Countess waved off her daughter on the hunt the next morning.

"But darling, I thought that you said that hunting was for old men," she commented as she stroked the mane of Moira's fine white mare. "Could it be that a young man has caught your eye?"

Moira blushed deeply and tried to hide her face.

'I must not be so obvious,' she decided. 'Mother will tell father and as I know nothing about this Stuart, he might not approve of my interest in him.'

"Why, mother, I declare I do not know what you are talking about," replied Moira, pulling on her mount's reins. "My only wish is to keep father happy and see how delighted he is that I am at last accompanying him on a hunt?"

The Countess looked over towards her beaming husband. He raised his stirrup cup in salute she had not seen him this happy in ages.

Moira spent the entire hunt doing her best to keep pace with Stuart, but his mount was much swifter than hers. He laughed as she struggled to keep up and waved as he sped off into the distance.

'He treats me as he would a younger cousin or little sister' she thought to herself dejectedly. 'Perhaps I am too young for him and he thinks me of no consequence.'

Later that evening she watched with a sinking heart as Stuart left before dinner with the rest of their guests. He thanked the Earl heartily for a wonderful weekend's sport and then inclined his head at Moira before kissing the Countess on the hand.

"Lady Strathcarron, it was a pleasure," he declared, his blue eyes sparkling.

Moira watched as Larry Harwood suddenly appeared at the top of the stairs. She thought what a contrast the two men presented. Larry, so lacking in social graces yet so sure of himself and Stuart, so charming and so self-effacing.

She hardly touched her dinner, she was thinking of Stuart. She also had to endure the ordeal of listening to Larry droning on and on about how easy it was to make money in America.

"You know, you could make a fist in New York, Scott!"

Moira shrank when he used her father's first name. She heard it rarely even her mother was not accustomed to using it much.

"*Make a fist?*" enquired the Earl clearly puzzled.

"It's an American expression – it means to make a success of something," Larry explained expansively. "With your breeding and eye for detail, you'd soon be one of the big bugs! Have you never thought of travelling to my country? There are Upstate mines just ripe for picking. The folks back home would sure give you a warm welcome with you being an Earl 'n' all!"

There was a glacial silence as Moira and her mother stared at the Earl in horror.

Surely he was not thinking of leaving them to go on a trip? Especially when things were so difficult on the estate.

Moira patiently waited for her father's dismissal of the subject, but to her dismay, none came.

"Mr. Harwood, my husband has much to occupy him here at Lednock," the Countess finally broke the silence, cool yet polite.

"Maybe you should come with him, Margaret. You'd love New York Society – it's every bit as high falutin' as anything you'd find in London. I don't expect you get much in the way of a social scene out here, do you?"

He took a deep drag on his cigar, oblivious to the *froideur* descending upon the room. Moira looked over at Ewen and could see that he was fuming.

The Countess simply rose gracefully from her chair and kissed her husband on the forehead.

"Dearest, would you mind if I excused myself? I am quite tired from all the excitement of the weekend. Ewen, Moira, goodnight."

"I think I will retire too," added Moira, eager to remove herself from the strained atmosphere.

Ewen grunted and jumped to his feet.

"Goodnight, father," he said and followed his mother and sister in silence.

As Moira made ready for bed, she thought about the weekend's events. Almost immediately, she pictured Stuart Weston so dashing in his hunting clothes with his hair flying out behind him. He really was a most unusual man.

She fancied that he was something like Alan Breck in Mr. Stephenson's novel '*Kidnapped*'. She had read it several times avidly and loved his descriptions of the troubles in the Highlands during the last century.

And what of Larry Harwood? A cold fear crept through her body as she remembered the conversation that had led to them all retiring early. Surely her father would not leave them?

"He cannot. *He cannot*!" she cried aloud, brushing her long dark hair ever more vigorously as if to expunge the thought from her head.

She found sleep did not come easily that night. She dreamt of Stuart only to have him evade her and then she dreamt that her father had left Lednock and sent word that he was never coming back.

But little did she know that worse was to come.

*

"There is a matter I wish to discuss with you all after dinner this evening," announced her father over breakfast. "Today I will be travelling to Stirling to see my lawyer but when I come back, I wish for everyone to be present."

"Does that include Mr. Harwood?" asked Ewen slyly.

"No, it does not. This is family business. Mr. Harwood will be dining with Lord Crieff this evening."

Ewen tried to conceal his delight, but Moira looked worried.

Later that morning as she accompanied him on his rounds of the farms, she expressed her concern.

14

"Ewen, I am certain that father is going to tell us something terrible. Do you know why he is going to Stirling today?"

"It is of some concern, aye, I agree," concurred Ewen, as he grappled with a late lamb. "But until we know what father has to say to us, we cannot worry unduly. He may be visiting his lawyer to amend his will. After all, our assets are considerably less now than when he first made it. I think that will be it."

"Yes," agreed Moira, "I hope you are right for all our sakes."

The day dragged by and Moira found it hard to keep herself occupied. She tried to finish her embroidery, but the light was not good enough on this overcast day for her to see well enough.

She then sought out her mother who was busy planning the week's meals.

"Our visitor is turning into an expensive drain on our resources," she sighed, checking the list of stores next to her meal plan and budget sheets.

"Did Mr. Harwood pay for the shoot?" enquired Moira.

"Yes, he did. But it will only cover some of the weekend's expenses. We must continue to be frugal, darling, if we are to make ends meet."

"Would it help if I sought some employment?" offered Moira, hesitantly. "I could teach at the local school or perhaps give dancing lessons."

"Darling, you are too kind but I could not consent to you lowering yourself. Remember, you are the daughter of an Earl and times are not so hard that we should be sending our children out to work as common servants."

"– or maybe I should think of getting married – "

Moira was picturing Stuart Weston as she spoke.

"Darling, you are so young and there will be plenty of time. Besides, what kind of dowry could we offer at the moment? No, dearest, you must stay at Lednock and pray that the harvest will be a good one. I heard Ewen saying only the other day that our potato crop is likely to be bountiful this year."

The door of the library flew open and there stood the Earl.

"Sir, I had not expected you for a few hours yet," smiled the Countess.

"Aye well, my business in Stirling was successfully concluded and so I hurried back home, anxious to see my dear wife."

Moira tactfully withdrew at this point, feeling that her parents would wish to be alone.

At last the gong sounded for dinner and everyone took their places. Moira noticed that her father did not touch the first course and only ate a small portion of the haddock. There was little conversation around the table.

Finally, after the pudding was taken away, the Earl cleared his throat.

"As you know, I requested that everyone be here for dinner tonight as I have a most pressing matter I wish to discuss."

He paused and then looked directly at his son.

"You may be pleased to hear that Mr. Harwood will be leaving us tomorrow to return to America and it is my intention to go with him."

There was an audible gasp from the Countess and Moira felt as if someone had gripped her throat.

"Father, you *cannot* leave us," cried Ewen, "we are only months away from the harvest and we need you here."

"Ewen, you have showed yourself to be more than capable of running the estate," replied the Earl, not meeting his eye, "I have every confidence that you will manage."

"But father, we need you," burst out Moira, tears starting to fill her eyes, "it is not just the estate, what about the castle and the village? If things go wrong for us this harvest, the farmers will be up in arms."

"Ewen will cope. He is a man and capable of doing a man's job."

"Dearest, what is the purpose of your visit to America?" The reasoned voice of the Countess broke through calm and collected.

"My dear wife, I have a chance there to make some money. Larry has assured me that whatever I invest will come back threefold if not more. I have realised some assets that I held in Stirling and with that money, I will go to America and come back much richer. I assure you, darling, I would not take an unwarranted risk, as well you know."

Moira could see that her mother was close to tears. The Countess simply nodded meekly and folded her napkin.

"Then there will be arrangements to make for your journey. I will speak to Rankin about the preparations first thing in the morning. Children, leave us now, please, I wish to speak to your father alone."

Both Ewen and Moira reluctantly rose and left the table. Moira could not hide the tears that were falling.

'I will go to him later and plead with him,' she mumbled as they made for the drawing room.

"I think he has made his mind up – you ken what father is like, he'll not be budged from his decision now that it's made," said Ewen, trying to comfort his sister as best he could.

And so later that evening, Moira went to her father and entreated him to stay.

"Please, father. If you are wanting to invest, then the shipyards of Glasgow are so much closer than America. Please, will you not reconsider?"

"You will mind your place, my daughter," the Earl snapped testily, "and that is not to question my decisions. The good book says to 'honour thy father and thy mother' and you will do just that. Have I made myself clear?"

"Yes, father," responded Moira, miserably retreating.

And so the next day dawned.

Although Ewen and Moira were glad that Larry was leaving them, the thought that he was taking their father with him was a very bitter pill indeed.

"It is for the good of Lednock Castle and the Strathcarrons," the Earl reminded them as he climbed into the carriage that would take him and Larry Harwood to Glasgow thence by steamer to Liverpool for their Atlantic crossing.

"Now, come and kiss your father and wish him '*bon voyage*'."

With sinking hearts, Ewen and Moira advanced towards the carriage to say their goodbyes. Moira clung to her father's neck and tried not to weep.

The Countess could hardly speak – she had not been parted from her husband for a single night since the day that they had wed.

"Goodbye, dearest," she called, waving as the coachman cracked his whip high over the heads of the team of horses. "Goodbye and God speed."

As the three of them watched the carriage speed down the drive, they all wept silently.

"Your father is doing this for the good of us all," said the Countess, hugging her two children close, "he will be back soon and Lednock shall stand proud once more."

"I do hope you are right, mother," replied Ewen, grimly, "our fate is now in his hands."

CHAPTER TWO

But the high hopes of the Strathcarron clan soon melted as the months wore on.

The Earl, never a man prone to putting pen to paper, wrote infrequently. When he did, he stated quite simply that he was in good health and that he was finding America a most exciting place.

"Well, that tells me nothing at all," groaned the Countess in exasperation throwing down the Earl's latest missive.

"What does father say?" enquired Moira eagerly.

"Look for yourself, darling. It is the usual, 'I am well and finding life in New York most stimulating'."

"Maybe he does not wish to raise our hopes unnecessarily."

"Or maybe there is nothing to tell. This really is too much. Your father has been away now for nearly five months and still no news of his investments – the very reason why he left us in the first place."

Ewen strode into the drawing room looking haggard and in need of a bath.

"News from father?" he asked wearily.

"Hardly," replied Moira sitting down on the worn velvet sofa. "He says nothing more than a few banalities."

"How go things on McKee's farm?" interrupted the Countess. She could see by Ewen's appearance that he had been up all night.

"We lost three more calves," he answered, flopping down on a wooden chair.

"I am certain that you are doing all you can," murmured the Countess soothingly. "If your father was here, he could do no more."

"Does he say when he is coming home?"

"I am afraid not, dearest. But he cannot stay in America much longer. It will be Christmas soon and I cannot imagine that he will want to spend it away from his family."

"I have some good news, mother," interjected Ewen, "we have recovered a substantial amount of the crop from the field of beet that was washed away two weeks ago when the burn burst its banks. There will be feed for the animals this winter if the weather stays fine and dries everything out."

"Well, we must be thankful for small mercies," she responded, casting her eyes heavenwards.

"Now, if you will excuse me, mother and Moira – I will bathe then sleep for a wee while before I go out again."

He rose yawning expansively.

The Countess and her daughter watched as he sauntered towards the stairs.

"He is a fine young man," whispered the Countess. "Your father would be so proud of him. He has had to cope with so much since he left – "

Moira could see her mother's eyes filling with tears, but she turned quickly away.

"Leave me now, my dear, I must go over the menus for cook."

Moira quietly closed the door of the drawing room behind her and made her way to the kitchen. Cook was making black bread – it had been some months since they had last tasted the white variety.

"Good morning, cook. What will you be serving us for luncheon today?"

Cook sighed and gestured towards the pile of swedes on the table.

"Neeps and tatties, my Lady."

Moira pulled a face. Times were hard indeed.

She loathed the plain fare that they were forced to eat nowadays, but she reminded herself that should her father come home with changed fortunes, then there would once more be meat for the table.

She slipped out of the kitchen door and into the vegetable garden.

She had not forgotten Stuart Weston, the charming stranger whom she had encountered there.

Indeed, she had caught a further glimpse of him in late September when he had ridden up to the castle to call on Ewen. She recalled each precious moment he had spent at Lednock, going over each second time and time again.

The way he had bowed and smiled at her, his hair falling wildly over his collar and the masterly fashion he sat astride his horse.

Twisting some strands of mint around her fingers, she inhaled the scent and thought wistfully,

'I do wish I had been bold enough to ask him to take tea with us. Surely it would not have been so unthinkably forward as he is an acquaintance of Ewen's?'

But she had not dared to ask and she felt only regret as the two men had set off, laughing heartily en route for the coast.

Moira had pleaded with Ewen to take her with him.

"What, a woman on board a ketch? *Unthinkable*," he roared.

Stuart, she noticed, did not join in the jocularity. Instead, he simply touched his hat and turned his horse towards the castle gates.

'He is so respectful and noble,' Moira had thought as she watched him canter off. 'I do hope that Ewen invites him to the castle again soon.'

But with all the troubles that had beset them, he had not come and so Moira's dream of becoming further acquainted with Stuart was yet one more whimsy to be dismissed, along with the idea of visiting Edinburgh.

Now, the weather had turned and it was November. The cold and rain descended on Loch Earn and Lednock had remained shrouded in clinging fogs.

The castle was a grim place in this kind of weather, its stone walls remaining chilly and damp.

It was on such a morning, towards the end of the month, that the telegram arrived.

Ewen was not at the castle – some tenant farmers had turned nasty upon hearing that their monthly rents were to be increased by three pence and he had gone to meet them.

Only Moira and her mother were at home.

Rankin walked in with his usual lack of urgency and handed the Countess the telegram. She caught her breath as she realised what it was.

"What is it, mother?"

"It's a telegram, darling. I think it is from your father."

"Do not tarry, open it."

The Countess held the telegram at arm's length, too nervous to open it in case it was bad news.

23

"Mother, we have to know what is inside. Pray, open it."

With a firm rip the Countess tore open the brown paper.

"What does it say? Oh, mother, do tell me, *tell me!*"

The Countess's eyes filled with tears, but they were tears of joy. Weeping, she handed the telegram to Moira.

"Darling, your father – he is coming home next Wednesday. He is safe and well, praise the Lord!"

Moira hastily scanned the telegram for some kind of clue as to her father's financial success – but found none.

Almost immediately, her joy was replaced by a creeping fear. If all was well, and her father had made his fortune, then surely he would have said as much in the telegram?

The Countess rang for Rankin and immediately began to pace the room.

"There is much to be done before your father's return. We must have the castle cleaned from top to bottom and ensure that there is meat for the table. I will order Ewen to have one of the pigs killed for the occasion – your father loves pork chops."

Rankin appeared, his creased face a mask of inscrutability. Moira had always been just the tiniest bit frightened of him as she found his manner quite threatening.

She had read Bram Stoker's '*Dracula*' and thought that if he had ever met Rankin, then surely he was the inspiration for the Count!

"Ah, Rankin. His Lordship is due home next Wednesday."

"Welcome news, my Lady."

"Indeed. Now, I want the entire castle spotless. Bring out the best silver and see that special attention is paid to the library."

Rankin hesitated for a second. Moira could see that something was troubling him.

"Are there any particular items of silver required?" he asked warily. There was an awkward silence during which Moira could have sworn that her mother had blushed.

"Just the platters and the cutlery, I think, Rankin. We don't want to overdo it?"

"Quite so, my Lady," he replied bowing deeply.

Moira was puzzled by this curious exchange. What had made Rankin and her mother so uncomfortable? Instinctively, she glanced towards the large mahogany display cabinet that housed the family silver. The shelves were almost bare.

'Where are the candelabra?' thought Moira, 'and that hideous Georgian oyster server that we usually fill with ice?'

Moira tried to give the gaping holes in the display cabinet no further thought.

*

Just before lunch Ewen returned from his meeting with the tenant farmers. Striding through the hallway, Moira walked straight into him.

She knew immediately that it had not gone well.

"Ewen, you surprised me."

"I am sorry, Moira, but I fear that I am in a foul temper. You cannot reason with these farmers – they seem not to understand that all our futures are in peril."

Moira watched her brother closely. He cared so much about the estate and had known all the tenants since he was a boy. He hated any kind of confrontation.

"Was it awful, Ewen?"

25

"Aye, ten men against one. They think we're being greedy, they don't know that we are *all* struggling."

Trying to raise Ewen's spirits, Moira told him the day's wonderful news.

"Ewen, you will not be struggling on your own for much longer father has sent a telegram and he arrives home next Wednesday."

For the first time in months – since his trip with Stuart Weston in fact – Ewen let out a joyous roar. He picked his sister up and twirled her around, hooting all the while.

"And the money, did he say anything about the money?"

"Not a word. He merely said that he was on his way home and to expect him on Wednesday."

"Then he'll be wanting to surprise us!"

Ewen's attitude was confident but Moira remained silent. Almost supernaturally, he seemed to divine what she was thinking.

"You think that all is not well too, do you not?"

"Yes. I confess that the lack of information has made me fear the worst."

Ewen walked away down the long hall, brooding all the while.

"If father had made money, then surely he would have sent some home by now?"

"He knew that if the harvest went badly for us, we would be in trouble. Although we've been lucky and it has been a fair one, things are still not easy."

"We should be more positive, Ewen," began Moira, after carefully considering what her brother had said. "Father is a modest man and would never be seen to flaunt himself or his money in any way. He may want to keep the surprise for us when he returns. A telegram is hardly private, after all – "

"Aye, maybe you are right, but let us promise each other that we will not tell mother of our misgivings."

"Of course, now away with you and get changed. Cook will not be pleased if we let our luncheon go cold – it's neeps and tatties."

Ewen pulled a face.

"Then the sooner father returns home, the better," he called, bounding up the stairs.

*

The news that the Earl's return to Lednock Castle was imminent spread through Loch Earn and the surrounding estates. Campbell, the farmer who had been one of the most outspoken over the rent increases, came to see Ewen.

Ewen was grooming his horse in the stables when the dour farmer appeared with his cap in hand.

"Campbell, what brings you to the castle?" asked Ewen, a little frostily.

"I hear that the Earl is due home this week, my Lord."

"Aye, that is so."

Ewen was quite taken aback by the man's uncharacteristically deferential demeanour. Campbell was a blunt crofter and often addressed Ewen by his Christian name.

"Then it will be a happy day for us all. I wanted to hear the truth from yourself – you will have no more trouble on our account."

Campbell put his cap back on and left. Ewen stared after him in disbelief. Had the hoary old crofter really come to

27

admit defeat? He wondered what other rumours were sweeping the village to have made a man such as he back down.

Ewen was still smiling to himself when he slipped in the back door – he wanted to avoid the scampering of the hired help who were busy making ready for the Earl's return.

In the kitchen, Moira was doing an inventory of the stores with cook. Ewen heard her voice and poked his head around the door.

A large, glazed ham sat on a dish while several brace of grouse hung from hooks overhead. There was butter and sugar aplenty and cook had made some oatcakes. Swiftly, Ewen snatched one and crammed it into his mouth greedily.

"Heir or not, I'll smack your hand if ye take one more," cook threatened, picking up a wooden spoon.

He gestured to Moira to come outside.

"What is it?"

"Campbell has just been to see me. He has conceded defeat over the rents."

"Father will be so proud of you," she said smiling. "You will have something positive to tell him on his return."

"Let us hope that he, likewise, brings good news."

The Countess, who had stepped into the kitchen, interrupted their conversation.

"What is this good news, pray?" she queried, raising an eyebrow.

"Mother, the farmers have accepted our new terms over the rents. Campbell came to see me this afternoon. I see that we are ready to celebrate – has father sent some money? I cannot see how else we could afford a whole ham!"

The Countess's face darkened and her hand rose to her throat. At first, Moira did not place any significance on the gesture, but as her mother stood there, she realised that her neck was not covered with her usual string of pearls.

'Surely she cannot have sold them?' Moira thought in horror.

She knew that the pearls had been a present from the Countess's father on the birth of Ewen. She could not imagine her parting with them.

But the ham, the sugar and the jars of gentleman's relish told another story.

'The sooner father gets home the better before we have to sell the castle as well.'

*

Moira could not have known how prophetic her words were to become. The day finally dawned of the Earl's return.

"I want today to be extra special," proclaimed the Countess as a huge vase of scented lilies was delivered.

"What time did father say he would arrive?"

Moira had come downstairs in one of her best dresses. Her hair was ornately done and she looked very grown up.

"Around five o'clock," replied the Countess. "We have all day to prepare."

Moira fervently hoped that her worst fears were not to be confirmed, but she soon found herself caught up in the preparations.

Five o'clock came all too soon. The Countess was flushed with excitement as she tidied her hair for the tenth time. Ewen and Moira sat in the drawing room, anxiously awaiting the sound of carriage wheels on the gravel outside.

Finally, just after the stroke of five, the Earl's carriage turned into the drive.

"Will you go outside to greet him?" asked Ewen quite pale with nerves.

"I cannot," whispered Moira. "In any case, we should let mother see him first."

"Aye," sighed Ewen, relieved.

The pair could tell by the shouts outside that their father was home.

There, standing in the hall looking in a most unpleasant humour was the Earl.

Moira thought that he looked older and thinner than when he had left and a cold feeling gripped her heart.

She ran to kiss him but he was gruff and dismissive.

"Let me get my coat off, girl," he snapped. Moira leapt back, feeling hurt.

'I have not seen my father in six months and he brushes me aside like a servant,' she thought, miserably. 'This does not bode at all well.'

Ewen strode up to his father to shake his hand.

"How went the harvest?" asked the Earl tersely,

"Not bad, father, not bad."

"Let us be grateful for small mercies," was the reply.

Ewen and Moira exchanged glances – any positive hopes they may have harboured were fast evaporating.

"Sir, would you care for some refreshment?"

The Countess was eager and solicitous.

"I just want to lie down awhile, woman. Can you not let me be? I am tired and will want dinner in an hour. I trust that will be possible?"

The Countess recoiled in horror – she did not recognise the man who stood there.

Collecting herself, she smoothed her hair and said to her children,

"Come now, your father is exhausted from his travels. We shall allow him to rest before dinner."

Moira and Ewen watched their father walk slowly upstairs without so much as a backward glance.

"This does not feel right," mumbled Ewen under his breath, "I have received warmer welcomes from the undertaker!"

*

And so dinner was a most sombre affair.

The Earl ate heartily of all that was put before him, relishing especially the pork chops, while the rest of the family did not. They scarcely dared to breathe for fear of upsetting him.

"How is the pork, dearest?" asked the Countess nervously.

"Aye, grand, grand," replied her husband, not looking up from his plate.

"What was the food like in America, father?" Ewen asked boldly.

"Good. Fine steaks – "

By the time the pudding arrived, the whole family were feeling tense.

Moira could tell that her father was building up to making some kind of announcement – she had seen him in this kind of mood before.

Not touching his Apple Snow, he cleared his throat. Everyone turned to look at him and the Earl began to speak,

"Much as I am glad to back in the bosom of my very dear family, it is with a heavy heart that I have returned to you."

He paused. Moira dug her fingernails deep into the palm of her hand, the blood rushing from her head.

"There is no easy way to say this, so I will say it simply. We are ruined, *utterly ruined*."

The table was silent, shocked into wordlessness.

"Larry Harwood was nothing but a crook who took our money and ran off with it. He promised me the earth and then did nothing but spend everything in a most profligate manner. He duped me into investing in a mine that did not exist and to secure the deal, I signed over the deeds to Lednock Castle and all the land.

"In short, we are penniless. Harwood has run off to heaven-knows-where and so the American Bank is calling in his debts. It is only a matter of time before they come to claim what is theirs. That being Lednock Castle."

Such was their shock that the family could not speak. Moira could see that Ewen was silently fuming in his chair and that her mother was trying not to cry.

In a strangled voice she broke the silence,

"But surely they cannot take our home? Scott, tell me that this is not so?"

"Would that I could, dearest Margaret, but I cannot. I have been an utter fool – how can you ever forgive me?"

The Countess patted his hand, tears spilling over.

"We will manage somehow. Ewen, Moira, would you please leave me and your father alone?"

"Yes, mother."

Outside the dining room, Ewen grabbed Moira by the hand and squeezed it hard.

She could not stop herself from weeping profusely.

"What will become of us, Ewen? Are we about to become homeless paupers?"

"Not while I draw breath, sister," came the grim reply. "We will overcome this."

"But father has lost the castle. Where will live? Where will we go?"

"I promise you, we will not be homeless," replied Ewen stoutly. "I will think of a way if I die trying."

"Perish that it comes to that, but never have we been in such peril! Oh, Ewen. What *will* become of us?"

CHAPTER THREE

Moira spent the whole night wide awake.

'I cannot believe that he would risk our home,' she muttered to herself over and over again as she tossed and turned.

She shivered as she tried to picture life away from the castle. Although she had often bemoaned its lack of modern conveniences and the numbing cold in the winter, she loved the castle with all her heart and could not imagine living anywhere else.

But in spite of her deep sorrow, her heart went out to her mother.

'Poor mother. She has so much to bear,' she pondered, as the dawn started to break over the castle battlements.

Feeling that it was useless to try and sleep now that the morning had come, Moira rose from her bed and began to brush her long, dark hair.

In the passageway outside, she could hear movement. Pulling on a robe, she slowly opened the door.

"Ah, Moira. Good morning."

It was Ewen.

"I could not sleep last night, Ewen. My head was simply spinning."

"Aye, mine too. Shall we take a walk along the brae before breakfast? I feel the need to take myself away from the castle for a while."

"Give me fifteen minutes and shall I meet you outside the kitchen garden?"

Ewen nodded and yawned. He had not shaved and there was a hint of red stubble appearing on his chin.

Fifteen minutes later, Moira had dressed and pulled on a pair of stout boots.

They were soon climbing up the hill behind the castle. The heather was deep underfoot and dew still clung to the blooms.

As they edged along the Loch, they both paused for a moment to look over the land that had been in the Strathcarron family for three hundred years.

Neither of them could believe that it was about to come to an end, and that some anonymous American bank may be about to inherit everything.

"What can we do, Ewen? We must take some action. I cannot bear to sit by and watch all this being taken away from us."

"Mary, Queen of Scots gave us this land," sighed Ewen, "and to think of it being owned by foreigners is heresy!"

"But father seemed certain that there was no way out. Father gave Harwood the deeds, Ewen."

"If I know father, the deed that Harwood has is merely a copy. Father is a canny man – not a buffoon. He would never have given him the real deeds. But I agree, we have to do something and without mother and father knowing – the shame would kill them if they thought that their children were trying to help them out."

Moira nodded in agreement. Their parents were fiercely proud and, as long as they lived under their roof, would never countenance their children providing for them.

"We could find jobs – "

"That would not save the castle, Moira."

"What about if we sold the estate off, farm by farm, before the creditors arrived?"

"No, we cannot."

"Or we could go and see father's lawyer and talk to him. Surely whatever he signed could not be binding outside America?"

"That is a good idea, Moira and aye, we should indeed pay Mr. Clooney a visit, but the best solution would be if we could buy father out of trouble."

Moira looked at her brother aghast.

"How could we do that? We have no private income and no assets."

"We could marry."

"And pray, how would that help?"

"Ah, if we both married rich spouses then maybe their families would be of a mind to help ours. It is a cruel injustice that father has brought upon himself, but an injustice nevertheless and many a fair-minded man would take up the cudgels on behalf of he who was wronged."

"But is that not for Mr. Clooney to attend to?"

"Mr. Clooney charges a crown to enter his office, where would we find the money to fight this through the courts?"

Moira remained silent – she was thinking of Stuart Weston. If she had to marry for money, then she would want her husband to be a man like him.

But how could she discover whether he had enough money to take them out of trouble? She resolved to find out through some devious feminine way, but she realised that now was not the time to broach the subject with Ewen. She must keep it to herself.

"Ewen, I am sure that mother has sold off the family silver the missing candelabra, the oyster bowl and there was that enormous pair of candlesticks."

"That would certainly explain the fine fare that graced our table when Harwood was staying. How I would like to get my hands on him! It makes my blood boil."

"I believe that mother has sold her pearls as well."

"Not the ones grandfather gave her when I was born?"

"Yes, the very same."

"Well, this is a fine business, Moira, I am afraid we have no alternative – marriage to a rich husband and wife it has to be."

"But I would feel as if I were selling myself," protested Moira angrily. She did not like all this talk of marriage for money as she wanted to marry for love and preferably Stuart Weston!

"It is either that or we end up living off the charity of relatives," replied Ewen dourly, "or worse still, the workhouse."

Moira could stand it no more. She ran away along the banks of Loch Earn and up onto the brae. Sobbing she threw herself onto a rock.

'I will not marry a man I do not love,' she wept pulling moss off the rock in anger. '*I will not*!'

Having followed her some way behind, Ewen appeared over the top of the brae and ran towards his sister.

"Don't fret, Moira, don't fret. Happen you'll meet someone you will fall in love with and he will be rich too. You have to see that this is our only course of action. I am not relishing wedding a girl for her money, but it is that or we face the consequences."

Moira dried her tears and sat down on the rock with her brother. The sun was climbing high in the sky and she realised that it must be way past breakfast time by now.

"You are right, Ewen, but how will we find these people? You have already met and discarded all the eligible young ladies hereabouts. And there is no one suitable in Edinburgh who is not either a toothless hag or a pan-faced wench."

Ewen began to laugh.

"You are too choosy, Ewen," continued Moira, "you have met some perfectly delightful young ladies over the past few years, but you deemed that none were good enough for you."

"Aye, well, that was before I was in dire need. No, sister, we need to look further afield than Edinburgh."

He paused and looked thoughtful as he continued,

"Where? Glasgow? Aberdeen? Please do not suggest Newcastle. London?"

"London!" cried Moira, looking shocked. "We cannot go to London. There is not the money and where would we stay?"

"I think that our dear friends the Cunninghams owe us a favour. It is indirectly because of them that we now find ourselves in this situation. We should write to them and tell them of our intention to take them up on their offer of hospitality. They know all the right people, they have rich friends aplenty. We could easily catch ourselves a pair of worthy spouses."

"I do not know. I will need to consider this idea at length."

"Well, don't tarry, sister, we have very little time."

Ewen helped his sister rise and held her hand tightly all the way back to the castle.

It was a gloomy greeting they encountered upon their return.

"Ewen and Moira. Where have you been?"

The Countess rushed towards them as they entered the hallway.

"We went for a wee walk, mother, nothing else."

"What is wrong, mother?" asked Moira sensing her disquiet.

"It is your father he has taken to his bed and refuses to get up. Ewen, I was hoping you might be able to persuade him of his folly."

"I will try, mother," he replied making for the staircase.

"You missed breakfast," said the Countess quietly as Ewen disappeared upstairs.

"Yes, I know. Neither of us slept at all well last night and we wanted to go for a long walk. I am sorry but we must have lost track of time. What is the time now?"

"Half-past ten. Cook will heat up some porridge if you ask her."

With a heavy heart, Moira took her leave and wandered off towards the kitchen.

"Ah, there ye are, my Lady!"

Cook was already reheating a saucepan of porridge on the iron range.

"And where is your brother?"

"He is with my father – "

"Aye, terrible business when a man like him takes to his bed," muttered cook stirring the porridge fiercely.

39

Moira wished that she had a friend to confide in. There was so much troubling her and she longed to discuss her private thoughts with a trusted friend someone – like Stuart perhaps.

But apart from the few acquaintances in Edinburgh whom she had not seen in over a year, there were no friends to be found on the estate. They had always been such a close family until the Earl had torn them apart and now Moira felt more alone than ever.

*

The Earl refused to come down from his bedroom and all of Ewen's pleadings seemed to fall on deaf ears.

A week passed and still the Earl remained steadfastly in his bed.

Ewen became restless. Now that he had decided upon a plan to help save the estate, he was eager to implement it. However, Moira had flatly refused to let him tell their parents, saying that until their father improved, they could not possible leave him.

"But Moira, every day we linger here brings us closer to being ejected from our home," howled Ewen in exasperation.

"Ewen, I understand but I fear for father. The shock of our plan could kill him."

"Darling sister, the shock of being evicted from his ancestral home is much more likely to kill him."

Moira thought long and hard on her brother's words and eventually, she conceded that he was right. They could not delay any longer Christmas was almost upon them and if they did not catch the round of Yuletide balls, they would have to wait until the spring. By which time, Lednock may be in the hands of Harwood's creditors.

So, the next day, Moira and Ewen told their mother of their decision.

"Heavens!" she reacted. "Why are you leaving us when we need you most? Ewen, Moira, I beg of you both, I need you here."

"But mother, would you stand in the way of us finding a solution to save the estate?"

"How so?" enquired the Countess,

"I cannot say, mother. But rest assured, the main purpose of this trip is not to make merry but to save the day. You must trust me – this is for the good of the family."

The Countess sank down onto the velvet sofa in the drawing room.

"London," she said, breathlessly, "and where will you stay? I will not have you accepting charity – "

"Mother, we would not dream of besmirching the family's reputation by begging," intervened Moira. "We will be staying with the Cunninghams. I will telegraph them presently. You may recall that when they stayed with us last year, they said we must return the visit – and so we intend to take them up on their kind offer."

The Countess considered Moira's words for a while.

"I will tell your father in my own time. Leave that much to me, please. Now, when do you intend to leave?"

"Very soon – possibly within the next few days," replied Ewen. "I have some business to attend to on the estate and then I will travel to Perth to call upon a friend of mine who may be in a position to help us with our journey South."

'Please let it be Stuart,' hoped Moira fervently. She had gleaned from subtly questioning cook that Stuart lived in Perth. Cook knew all the locals from Stirling to Dundee – she had worked in many grand houses in the past.

"Who would that be?" she demanded of her brother.

"He is an old friend – don't worry, we will not be in the hands of brigands."

"All the same, I wish to be assured of your sister's safety," interrupted the Countess. "I trust this friend is known to us?"

"He is, aye," answered Ewen mysteriously.

Later that afternoon Moira and Ewen discussed their plans as they took a turn around the grounds.

"Aye, we will need a substantial amount of money," Ewen declared. "It is not just keeping the creditors at bay that concerns me. The castle is in urgent need of repair."

Moira gazed up at the turrets and the battlements. Lednock had been built in the style of the much older castle that had once stood there. To the untrained eye, the castle looked fourteenth century at least, when it was in fact built in the sixteenth century.

"This place has so many memories," she murmured. "Should someone else live here, it would feel as if all the happy times we spent here would vanish into nothingness."

"No, I keep my memories in here, "replied Ewen thumping his heart. "But it's true, every stone, every window has a tale to tell, and to never stand here and look over the Loch. Why, it would be unthinkable!"

"Ewen, I worry so for our father. It is not right that a man his age should take to his bed. Mother says that he has hardly eaten and I fear for his health and sanity."

"He is of sound mind yet," countered Ewen angrily. "Our father is not mad simply because he made a wrong decision. Have a care how you speak about him."

Moira felt ashamed of herself, but even so, she felt deeply resentful that her father had jeopardised the family's security on what she perceived to be a whim.

As they both walked to the stables in silence, she finally spoke up,

"It is mother I worry for too, Ewen. If the worst came and we were evicted from the castle, you and I would surely survive somehow. We would be able and willing to work for others, but mother – she has never worked and would not countenance living off the charity of well-meaning relatives. How would she survive?"

Ewen stroked his stallion's head. The horse had heard his voice and had put his fine chestnut head out of his stable door.

"I will miss you, Sturrock," he crooned, caressing his ears and mane. "But I will return soon I promise you."

"Ewen, the horses! We would lose them too should Lednock be repossessed."

Moira thought of her mount Jessie, a doughty, bay mare. The horse had been a present from her father when Moira was just thirteen and the pair had become firm friends. She knew she could not bear to part with her.

"Then all the more reason for us to travel to London and resolve this delicate matter," muttered Ewen.

He loved his Sturrock every bit as much as Moira loved Jessie.

As the two made their way back to the castle, they were dismayed to see a black carriage standing by the front entrance.

Moira grabbed her brother's arm, feeling quite faint.

"Ewen, surely it is not the creditors already."

She felt hot and sick. A man dressed all in black climbed out of the carriage. He was carrying a large folio and held the air of one who was on official business.

"Come, sister, we must see what brings this man to the door of the Strathcarrons."

Ewen strode off in front of her, his expression grim.

'Please do not let it be the creditors,' she prayed, as she reluctantly followed him. Fear gripped her heart and made her legs feel curiously unstable.

By the time she had made her way to the drawing room, she could hardly breathe.

The Countess was seated and was reading some kind of document, whilst the tall thin man in black stood by the fireplace.

Ewen wore an angry expression and was remonstrating with the man as Moira walked in.

"But this is outrageous," he was saying. "How can that be?"

"Mother, Ewen, what is it?" she enquired nervously.

"Darling, do not be alarmed. This gentleman has come to serve us notice to complete an inventory of the estate. That is all. It does not mean that our departure from here is imminent."

"And I say it is the business of no man how many horses or pairs of boots I own," erupted Ewen.

"Darling, the gentleman is not asking for a list of the contents of your wardrobe," answered the Countess calmly.

"My Lady, I will return in a month's time to see that it has been completed. You will receive more instructions forthwith. I will see myself out."

The man buckled up his folio and gave a short bow. Turning on his heels, he nodded to Ewen and Moira before leaving the room.

It was all too, too much for the Countess. She broke into sobs, crumpling up the form for the inventory in her hand.

Ewen rushed to his mother's side to comfort her.

"Does father know about this?"

"Not yet."

"We must keep this development from the servants. Should they find out, they will panic and leave us."

The Countess blew her nose on her lace hanky and nodded in agreement.

"You are wise, darling. I think it is best if we maintain that we have had a visit from a representative of Mr. Clooney. We do not want servants' gossip making this whole unseemly affair even worse."

"Yes, mother," replied Moira, "shall I speak to Rankin?"

"No, I will see him later when I am feeling more able. I must first go and break the news to your father."

"Mother, there is no need to bother him with such a trifle. I will take care of it."

Ewen pulled himself up to his full height with a steely glint in his eye. The Countess regarded him with pride such a fine son.

Moira hastened over to where her mother sat and took the place next to her.

45

"Mother, how is father today?"

"Much the same," came the reply. "He eats not enough to keep a bird alive and refuses to leave his bed. Nothing I say to him seems to lift his spirits. I have yet not dared tell him that you are going to London."

"Mother, we have to go. If there is a chance that we can find a way to save the estate, then we must take it."

"Yes, I know. I understand that it is a selfless thing that you are doing. It is not as if you are out hunting for a sweetheart or some other such frivolity."

Moira could not stop from blushing. She bowed her head, hoping that her mother would not see her embarrassment.

"And the Cunninghams are such good people," continued the Countess, "but mind you do not tell them of our current predicament. I do not want our family name being dragged through the rumour mill of London I would die of shame."

"Of course I will not breathe a word. There is no need for Lady Cunningham to know of our present circumstances. I fail to see what business it can be of hers."

The Countess sighed deeply and looked around the drawing room.

On every wall hung paintings of the Strathcarrons – from the first Earl to her husband's father. There were engravings of hunts and horses, bronzes of foxes and eagles, sabres and shields – all reminders of the Strathcarrons' illustrious past.

"There have been Strathcarrons at Loch Earn since medieval times," she reminisced. "Those were war torn days and it seems that now we are facing equal strife. However, this time it is not a hoard of marauders at the door but the proverbial wolf."

Moira rose and left her mother to her thoughts.

Heading upstairs, she felt a chill wind blowing and shivered.

Was it an omen of events to come?

*

It was with a very heavy heart that Moira began to gather up her clothes to pack into the three trunks that now stood in her room.

As she began to pull her ball dresses out of the wardrobe, she saw them with fresh eyes. Her apricot chiffon now appeared dowdy rather than being the comfortable favourite of old. She had worn it for the last two Seasons in Edinburgh and she suddenly feared that it would look positively old-fashioned compared to the Socialites of London.

'This will never do,' she told herself, looking at the too-full skirt and fussy detailing on the yoke. 'I will look like a simple country girl, rather than a sophisticated young lady of good birth.'

In despair, she threw it onto the bed. But what else was there?

A white linen dress suitable only for summer wear, a lavender silk that resembled half-mourning and a pale blue taffeta that was tailored for a much younger girl.

'How will I ever find myself a husband wearing these?'

Just then, her mother knocked on the door. Entering, she found a tearful Moira miserably discarding dress after dress.

"Darling, what is wrong?"

"Mother, how will I be able to hold my head up at a London party in any of these? They are so out of date. I cannot possibly embarrass the Cunninghams by attending balls wearing any of them."

The Countess looked at her sadly,

"But we cannot possibly afford to buy you new ones and there is not time anyway. You are leaving so soon."

Moira winced at her gentle reproach.

It was true, they were spending money they did not have by visiting London – Ewen had talked of selling a couple of fine horses to pay for the trip. There would certainly be no money left for such luxuries as new gowns.

"Dearest, maybe these will help to take the attention away from the fact that your dresses are not the height of Paris fashion."

The Countess handed Moira a pale blue box. She opened it and inside glinted a diamond necklace and earrings.

"Mother. I cannot take them!"

"They are just a loan and if you take them to London, I should not be tempted to sell them. They were your grandmother's and are quite valuable. Be sure to guard them well and ask Lady Cunningham to put them into her safe as soon as you arrive." Moira hugged her mother close, tears in her eyes.

"Mother, thank you. I will miss you so much."

"And I you, my dearest. Now dinner will be served in half an hour – I will ask Rankin to sound the gong,"

Her mother slowly left the room, pausing only to throw a glance at her daughter.

'She is so young and vulnerable,' thought the Countess, 'I do hope that Lady Cunningham will protect her from unsavoury advances. Moira may not be such a stunning beauty, but she has a most appealing comeliness that is bound to attract the wrong kind of attention.'

Dinner was indeed a sombre affair.

The Earl took soup and bread in his room, refusing all meat. Ewen ate a little while Moira pushed her rabbit stew around the plate.

"Not hungry?" asked her mother anxiously.

"No, mother," she replied, not daring to tell her that she detested rabbit stew. She was looking forward to eating decent food again at the Cunninghams. Almost immediately, she chided herself for having such disloyal thoughts.

"I will be leaving early tomorrow morning for Perth," announced Ewen suddenly.

"I intend to arrange our passage South."

"Is it Mr. Weston you are seeing?" ventured Moira, her heart beating wildly.

"Aye, it is."

"Will you say I was asking after him?"

Ewen eyed his sister suspiciously for a moment.

"Ah, I remember. You met him at the hunt when Harwood was here, didn't you?"

"Yes, he helped me – when Jessie stumbled down a hole near Campbell's farm – " stammered Moira feeling embarrassed. It was a lie but she felt it necessary to conceal her true feelings from her brother.

"Aye, he is ever the gentleman is Stuart Weston," commented Ewen and then appeared to lose interest in the subject, much to Moira's relief. "Now, mother, if you will excuse me, I should retire to bed now."

The Countess sighed heavily and folded her napkin.

"He has so much responsibility, it is not right that he has to endure such a burden."

"Mother, he is more than capable. Do you not think he has shown himself to be a worthy son and heir during all our troubles?"

"Of course, but he should not be so weighed down. Ewen is nearly twenty-three and he should be searching for a bride, not worrying about the future of the estate."

Moira blushed. If only her mother knew the true reason for their journey to London!

"I will bid you goodnight too, mother."

In the solitude of her room, Moira made ready for bed. As she brushed her long, dark hair, she regarded herself in the mirror.

'Will I be pretty enough to attract a rich husband?' she worried. 'There will surely be much more beautiful ladies than I in London. Who is to say that I will be lucky enough to make the right kind of match?'

She sighed and put down her silver brush. It bore the crest of the Strathcarrons – a bear and two crossed sabres – and she stroked it lovingly.

'I must be prepared to marry a man I may not love and because of his riches rather than his charms.'

Looking once more at her reflection in the mirror, a cold fear gripped her heart. She knew that deep down, not marrying for love would be a living death for her.

She could not stop the tears from flowing as she sank down onto the dressing table and sobbed her heart out.

'Oh, I wish I had never been born to endure these terrible, terrible days. What will become of all of us?'

CHAPTER FOUR

The next day, Ewen was up and out of the house before dawn broke. Outside, there was a layer of frost on the ground and even he found the air rather bracing.

Having slept only lightly, Moira awoke as soon as she heard the sound of hooves resounding on the stones.

It was just gone midday before Ewen arrived back in the family carriage.

Moira ran down to meet him.

"What news, my brother," she enquired anxiously, "was your business successfully concluded?"

Oh, how she longed to ask him for news of Stuart. But she dare not her brother would not be happy about her harbouring affection for anyone who may not prove to be suitable husband material.

"Aye, it was," he replied, "we are due to leave this evening for Dundee. We will be sailing on the next available tide."

"Sailing? I had thought we would be travelling by train."

"You will find the journey more pleasant and private by sea," he answered, "and it is cheaper, mind. A friend of mine has been kind enough to offer us passage to Tilbury and then we will travel by carriage on to the Cunninghams. Has her Ladyship acknowledged your telegram yet?"

"Yes, a reply arrived about an hour ago. She is delighted and says she cannot wait to entertain us. We are arriving in the midst of some most enchanting parties apparently."

"All the better for capturing our quarry!"

"Ewen, do not speak of our mission so, you make it sound so cold-blooded."

"God willing, it will be a pleasant diversion," responded Ewen, sitting down and pulling off his boots. "But we must be prepared for it to be a chore. I loathe dancing parties. Give me a fine hunt any day."

"Tell me more about the ship. How long will the journey South take?"

"Kelpie says three or four days depending upon the weather. If the going is rough, then it may take a week."

'Kelpie?' thought Moira, her heart sinking with disappointment, 'so it is not Stuart's ship we shall be sailing on after all.'

All Moira's fond dreams of a romantic voyage with Stuart were instantly shattered. And she had so hoped it would be his vessel they would be taking.

"So what kind of ship is it we are taking?"

"It is one powered by steam. Quite new, I understand. They are fast overtaking the old sailing ships of yore, Kelpie tells me. He has a house nearby, but prefers to be on the open sea. You could say it is a hobby of his – he takes any kind of cargo – goods, animals, passengers – "

"So, we are to share a berth with a herd of cows, are we?" exclaimed Moira.

"No. This trip is for two-legged cargo only."

"I do not care to remain in Dundee overnight, Ewen. It is such a rough city. We had better not tell mother we intend to stay there overnight as she knows it from her girlhood and has naught but ill to say about the place."

"It's not that bad, Moira. When mother lived there, it was a much rougher city. The jute and linen industry has made it far more civilised. And it's where Mr. Keiller makes his famous jams and marmalade."

"Even so, are we not able to journey straight to the ship. What is it called?"

"The *Victorious.* The tide is quite unpredictable in the mouth of the Tay, so we are best advised to stay overnight and wait for word to be sent when it is time to sail."

As well as being bitterly disappointed that the ship did not belong to Stuart, Moira felt nervous at the prospect of staying in Dundee. In spite of her brother's reassurances, the thought filled her with dismay.

Ewen stood up, his boots in hand.

"I have asked the stables to make the carriage ready for five o'clock. I do not expect it will take us more than four hours to reach Dundee."

Moira returned to her room and resumed her packing.

'I have so many things to take with me,' she mumbled, having filled two trunks already with an enormous pile of clothes still lying waiting on the bed.

She picked up the blue box that contained her mother's diamonds and opened it.

The jewels sparkled in the pale afternoon sun that was streaming through the mullion windows.

'Perhaps they will bring me luck,' she thought, 'they will certainly enhance my appearance. If only I was not so sure that I am going to look like a silly Scottish simpleton. I would certainly fade into the background without the addition of these.'

Fastening the necklace around her throat, she regarded her reflection and decided that yes, the diamonds did indeed lend her a most engaging air.

'They will have to be *the bait* to land my prize catch.'

But it was Stuart, always Stuart whom she pictured herself with, arm-in-arm at some glittering ball, strolling through Hyde Park or visiting the British Museum.

It was Stuart, who in her mind's eye accompanied her to the Fountain restaurant in Fortnum and Mason for tea.

'I must set aside these ridiculous dreams,' she thought, getting quite cross with herself for fantasising so shamelessly. My duty is to help save father from ruin and if marrying a rich man is the only way, *then so be it*.'

Throwing the last of her belongings into the third trunk, she carefully hid the jewels in her vanity case that she would carry with her everywhere.

'I must not let father and mother down,' she told herself once more as if to convince herself. 'In this enterprise, my personal wishes count for nothing.'

*

Around four o'clock, the Countess knocked on Moira's door.

Moira was pleased that her mother had come to her for a private chat before she left. She would miss her terribly.

"Are you quite ready, dearest?" asked the Countess, looking at her daughter affectionately.

"Yes, mother, I am."

"Your father has requested that you go and see him before you leave."

"You have told him?"

"Yes, I have. He took the news quietly. He is not a man to show much emotion."

Moira nodded, her father was quick to anger but slow to display love or affection or concern. Her mother was the complete opposite the Countess wore her heart on her sleeve. Especially where her beloved children were concerned.

"I need not repeat that you must not tell anyone in London of our predicament," she began hesitantly.

"Of course not, mother."

"If people hear that we are in trouble, our name will be mud and we will be cut off from polite Society. It will ruin your chances of eventually making a good match"

"Mother!" cried Moira, blushing once more.

Her mother, however, took her embarrassment as a sign of modesty.

"Darling, you will wed one day. But there will be time enough and when the day comes, hopefully we shall find ourselves in better circumstances."

The Countess hugged her daughter close, stroking her hair.

"You must not worry about what is happening here," she whispered, "you go with our blessing this might be the last chance you have of enjoying yourself and you must seize it."

Moira began to weep softly into her mother's warm bosom. She smelt faintly of lavender and cotton starch – homely comforting smells that she would miss.

"I must hurry to father now," she said, taking her leave. "I am most anxious to see him before we depart."

Walking down the corridor to her father's room, she was filled with dread.

She opened the door and found the room in darkness the heavy curtains were pulled and only the tiniest chink of light was filtering through.

Her father was asleep but she decided to wake him.

"Father, father," she called gently.

"What is it?" he muttered still half asleep.

"Father, we shall be leaving shortly to go to London. I am here to say goodbye."

Just then the door opened and her brother strode in.

"Ewen, is that you?"

"Yes, father."

"You have come to bid me goodbye too?"

"Yes, I promise you I will return and that things will improve."

"I cannot see how that will be," he sighed, "but you go with my blessing. God speed and come home soon, son."

The Earl put out his hand and grasped Ewen's, gripping it hard. Tears sprung into Ewen's eyes – this was the nearest his father ever came to affection.

"Farewell, father," Ewen and Moira cried.

"Farewell."

Downstairs was a hive of activity. Rankin gave orders to the footmen to take the luggage out to the waiting carriage, while cook thrust a picnic box into Moira's hands.

"It's no much," she said, "just a few oatcakes and some cheese. An apple or two and some dried pork."

Moira had never travelled beyond Edinburgh before and never on the open seas.

As well as being excited, she was also terrified.

Climbing up into the carriage, Moira tried to record every last detail of Lednock's walls and turrets in her mind, for she did not know when she would see them again.

"Are you ready, sister?" asked Ewen, gripping the sides of the carriage.

"Yes, I am."

Slowly the horses pulled forwards and the carriage began to move.

Moira, blind with tears, waved out of the window until they reached the gates.

"Goodbye, mother and father," she whispered. "The next time we see you, we will have the means to save the estate."

"Aye, but we must not count our chickens yet," grunted Ewen grimly. "We have no way of knowing what lies ahead."

Moira looked at her brother closely – he was quite pale, his gaze fixed firmly on the way ahead.

"Well, we're on our way."

"Do you think we shall succeed in our quest?" Moira asked tremulously.

"We have to. That much is certain."

"How shall we find these spouses?"

"I'll warrant that the Cunninghams know many people. You mentioned parties, no doubt we will be the novelty at them. The Cunninghams will wish to show us off to their friends. You must be prepared to feel like an exhibit at the zoo, Moira, but we must bear it willingly."

Moira studied her brother closely. He was handsome enough but not the most sociable of men. He was far happier in the company of his own sex and apart from her thought most women to be silly creatures.

"You will have to learn to make polite conversation, Ewen, and not to be rude to the young ladies you will meet. They will be used to fine London ways and not our rough Highland manners."

"You make me sound like a bear in a cave. I promise you, I will be on my best behaviour at all times. That much I can guarantee."

"And you will dance?"

"If I have to."

Moira could see that her brother was gritting his teeth as he spoke. She thought it wise to change the subject.

"I must confess, Ewen, that I am concerned about sailing on the open seas. The nearest to the sea I have ever been was a pleasure cruise in the Firth of Forth."

Ewen could not help smiling. His sister was always so brave and strong. Yet she had a vulnerable streak.

"It is the same, but the difference being you will not see the banks of the Forth."

"Ah, but you have been on Stuart Weston's ship, have you not?"

"Aye, many a time."

There was a break in the conversation while Moira deliberately waited to see if Ewen would reveal more about Stuart. But he did not.

'Ewen does not understand the subtleties of women,' she told herself smiling.

The carriage rattled on into the night and soon, Moira was rocked to sleep.

It was nearly ten o'clock by the time that they reached the outskirts of Dundee.

"Wake up, Moira. We are almost there."

Moira yawned and stretched.

"Where will we stay?"

"There is a small, respectable lodging house not far from the port," replied Ewen, "Mrs. McRae is the landlady. I have sent word ahead that we would be arriving late so she is expecting us."

At last they drew up beside a tall house made from very square stones. Ewen rapped on the brass knocker and waited.

Presently a small round woman of about fifty answered the door. She was wearing an old-fashioned mobcap and a shawl. She peered out into the darkness at Moira and then beckoned.

"Ye'll come in quietly. Ye must not disturb my other guests."

Moira shuddered as they entered the cold hallway. The carriage took off for the port to take their luggage to the *Victorious*. Clutching her vanity case containing her jewels, Moira followed Mrs. McRae upstairs.

The woman handed her a lit candle stub as she opened the door.

"Here ye are now, I'll bid ye goodnight. Sir, follow me your room is nearby."

Moira walked in and immediately she sensed the smell of damp.

Wrinkling her nose, she felt the quilt on the bed – it was hard and the filling had compacted and it would afford her very little warmth tonight.

But she was so tired that she did not undress. She simply slid underneath the old quilt and fell asleep.

She slept badly. The house creaked all night long and was fiercely cold. After only a few hours sleep, Moira had awoken stiff and freezing.

Creeping downstairs, Moira heard the clock in the dining room chime seven.

"Ah, good morning, miss. Breakfast is on the table."

Mrs. McRae disappeared down the dark corridor. Ewen was already at the table, drinking a cup of tea.

Moira stared in horror as two thin slithers of cold toast greeted her. She held one up and grimaced.

"Aye, I know. Do you have anything left of cook's provisions?"

"I left the picnic box in the carriage. They will have loaded it onto the ship."

Ewen let out a long sigh. He would have been glad of oatcakes and cheese right now, even if they had only a few left from the journey.

"I nearly broke a tooth on my toast," he whispered as Moira sipped her cold tea.

She was too busy thinking of what life would hold for them should they lose the estate. Cold toast for breakfast, no heat, using candles down to the wick and quilts that had seen better days.

The thought made her want to cry and it was all she could do to hold back the tears. Her clothes felt dirty and her hair was a mess. It had been too dark in her room to tidy it and her carefully coiled chignon was now in danger of unwinding.

Ewen yawned and stretched.

"Don't worry, sister. We shall soon be on our way."

Just as he spoke, there was a loud rapping at the front door. Mrs. McRae appeared in the hall and opened it. Shuffling into the room, she handed Ewen a note.

"This is for ye."

"Ah, this must be from Kelpie."

He hastily read the note and nodded,

"Aye, it is. We sail at ten o'clock this morning. We should be ready to leave shortly."

They left Mrs. McRae's grim establishment gladly. Ewen handed over a few shillings and was glared at for his trouble.

Not far from the docks they hailed a lone carriage and continued their journey in relative comfort.

The thin sun had risen and Moira found herself shivering. However, she was pleased to see that there was very little wind their passage should be smooth today.

All around them, porters bustled to and fro and in the distance, Moira could see the giant whaling ships moored. They dwarfed every other vessel in the port.

"There," shouted Ewen, "that is the *Victorious*."

Moira looked to where her brother was pointing. It was a squat, iron-clad ship that he was waving at. She thought that it looked ugly in comparison with some of the old clippers that gracefully rocked in their moorings.

Ewen helped Moira up the narrow gangway. Underneath their feet, she could hear the roar of engines.

"Surely we are not moving so soon?" she asked.

"No, it will be Kelpie testing the engines. We have a long journey ahead of us and it would never do for them to stop working halfway to Tilbury."

Moira felt decidedly unsteady as they walked along the decks. The fresh sea air whipped her hair loose from its pins and it tumbled down around her shoulders.

"I hope my cabin has a mirror," she exclaimed, trying to coil her hair back onto her head hurriedly. It would not do for her to be introduced to Stuart's friend with her hair flowing freely.

"Come, let us see if we can find Kelpie. I'll warrant he's busying himself down below, he's a man who likes to get his hands dirty."

He led Moira through some doors and down a steep set of stairs and thence through a warren of corridors that all looked the same.

Finally after proceeding further down into the bowels of the ship, Ewen bade Moira to wait outside for him whilst he entered the engine room.

"It is no place for a lady," he explained, "too dirty and noisy and I no want the stokers feasting their eyes on you."

Ten minutes later, Ewen emerged hot and sweaty from the engine room.

"My friend will join us in the Saloon upstairs. He says that there is a cold breakfast ready for us. Come, sister, I am famished and thirsty."

The two of them made their way up on deck to the Saloon – it was a tastefully furnished room that boasted many comforts of home. Moira looked appreciatively at the elegant chairs and furnishings. The buffet table was laden with white bread cut into thick slices, butter, jams and marmalades.

"White bread," shouted Ewen, rushing over to pick up a slice. Without waiting to butter it, he bit into the thick dough – his face a picture of ecstasy.

"Mmm! Moira, you have to taste this. It's fresh and still warm."

Moira eagerly took a slice and buttered it. She could not decide which jam to put on it and so chose marmalade instead. As the thick, sweet jelly hit her tongue she thought it the most delicious taste.

"Ah, I see that you are availing yourself of my hospitality. Pray, continue."

"Kelpie!"

Moira turned, her mouth full of bread and marmalade, to see none other than *Stuart Weston* standing there grinning at her!

She was so surprised that she could have choked. She was highly embarrassed that he had caught her with her mouth full.

"Moira, I believe you two have already met?" asked Ewen mischievously.

"But I thought you said your friend was called Kelpie?"

"Aye, it's his nickname."

"I should explain," put in Stuart, "that when I was a wee boy, I looked just like an imp and so everyone called me 'Kelpie'. It is a name that has stuck."

"I would prefer to call you Stuart – " said Moira, haughtily. She had no time for such childish games.

"As you please," agreed Stuart smiling.

'I cannot believe it is he,' Moira thought, as Stuart and Ewen talked together animatedly. 'Such good fortune and now I shall have ample time to enquire into his means and see if he might indeed make me the match I need to keep everyone happy.'

Her mind was whirling as Stuart showed her to her cabin.

Away from Ewen, he became quiet and deferential. Moira noticed that he had cut his hair a little and she was not sure that she liked it. She much preferred his dashing cavalier style.

"Now, madam."

"Please, you must call me Moira."

"Very well, Moira, here is your cabin. I trust you will be comfortable here but should you require anything, I am sure I can oblige."

He made a little bow and smiled, his pale blue eyes sparkling. They were so penetrating that Moira felt as if they could read her most private thoughts.

"Would you care to see around the *Victorious* once you have settled in?"

"Why, yes. I would love to," replied Moira demurely, suddenly feeling giddy.

"Very well. Perhaps you would meet me on the bridge in half an hour?"

"I could be ready earlier," said Moira eagerly.

"Fifteen minutes it is then," Stuart bowed once more and left her cabin.

'How handsome he is,' she said to herself with glee. 'So dashing and charming. I shall never want this voyage to end.'

She quickly unpacked one of her trunks and carefully hid her vanity case containing her diamonds.

'I must enquire if there might be a safe or deposit box on board so that I can be sure of their safety,' she thought.

In order to look at herself in the square mirror on the wall, Moira had to stand on tiptoe to do her hair. She decided that a chignon was too severe and dressed her hair in a more becoming style.

'I must change my dress,' she decided, looking in dismay at what she was wearing. 'I do not wish to appear tired and ill-kempt in front of Stuart.'

Pulling a green woollen day dress from her trunk, she was annoyed to see how crumpled it looked.

'This will have to do,' she sighed, 'it is a pretty colour on me and I doubt that Stuart will notice the creases.'

Stuart was waiting for her on the bridge, munching on a piece of bread.

"Ah, Moira! Enchanting," he greeted her, his eyes coolly appraising her.

"Thank you. I feel so much better now that I have had a chance to wash and change. Our lodgings left much to be desired."

"Well, I hope that your current ones meet with your approval?"

Stuart was as charming as she remembered from their first encounter in the garden although she still felt that perhaps he viewed her merely as Ewen's little sister.

"Yes, yes, most suitable. I am looking forward to my first night at sea. I do hope I will not be seasick."

"I think you will find tonight's passage a smooth one.

There is but a slight wind and the ship's engines will make light work of the going," Stuart reassured her.

"That is well as I am afraid of becoming ill, this being my first sea voyage." She blushed and hung her head. Stuart must think her a very silly girl indeed.

But he gave no indication of his thoughts. Instead, having finished his snack he led her from the bridge and onto the deck.

He showed her every inch of the ship and patiently explained all the nautical terms. However, Moira was only half listening.

'What a fine profile he has,' she thought to herself, as Stuart explained the difference between port and starboard. 'And I declare I have never seen such startling blue eyes.'

But Stuart seems oblivious to her interest. Everything he said, each gesture he made, was courteous yet a little detached. Moira had been wooed by the young men she had met in Edinburgh and she could tell that Stuart's manner was far from that of an ardent admirer.

'Ah, but he would not wish to behave in an improper fashion,' she told herself.

Moving back to the Saloon, Stuart bade Moira sit down in one of the comfortably upholstered chairs.

"Such luxury," she remarked, sinking into the feather cushion of an easy chair. "This room is truly a home from home."

"No, it is much more homely than my own house," replied Stuart, shaking his head. "I have a home in Perth but it is somewhat lacking. I do not have the money to make the necessary renovations. It is only a modest abode, but my income is not sufficient to maintain it."

Moira's disappointment was palpable.

All her fond fantasies of her search for a husband ending on board the *Victorious* began to crumble. If Stuart was not rich enough to pay for some mere renovations to a modest house, he was in no position to help her family. With a sinking heart, she realised that her silly romantic notions about him must be forgotten.

"I think I shall return to my cabin," said Moira, suddenly feeling the need for solitude.

"Very well. We shall be sailing very soon, so you will be undisturbed. Luncheon will be served at one o'clock in the Saloon, but if you should feel unwell, I can ask the cabin boy to bring something below."

Feeling morose, she returned to her cabin and lay down on the bunk.

'Why, oh, why could not Stuart Weston have enough money,' she called to the Heavens. 'It is quite unfair that I meet a man who is so right in every other way – yet who appears to have barely enough funds for his own outgoings. *It is so unfair.*'

She hit her pillow with her fists and began to cry.

'He is so handsome and so kind too. If I am honest, I do not want to marry a man I do not love.'

The ship's engines began to turn over and Moira felt a jolt.

'So, we are on our way and our mission begins – the search for a suitable husband. But, why, why could that not be Stuart? I dare not fall in love with him. Ewen would never forgive me.

'Truly fate has dealt me a poor hand. But for the sake of my father and Lednock Castle, I must endure it.'

Even so the thought made her weep profusely until finally she fell asleep.

CHAPTER FIVE

The next day dawned bright and clear with a calm sea. Moira awoke and, feeling disorientated, took several minutes to remember where she was.

At first, she thought she was still asleep and in a dream and then she realised that she was on board the *Victorious* bound for Tilbury and London.

With a chill, she remembered the previous day's events and shuddered to recall how she had cast longing eyes in Stuart's direction.

'How could I be such a little fool?' she asked herself. 'Much as I am drawn to him, I must forget any such stupid ideas. He has not the financial wherewithal and that *must* be a man's most potent attribute in order to qualify as a suitable husband.'

Moira entered the Saloon some twenty minutes later to be greeted by a generous spread for breakfast. Ewen was already seated and tucking into kippers and eggs.

"Good morning, sister. How are you this fine day? You look a wee bit pale."

"I am fine, dearest," she replied, helping herself to a pair of kippers.

Ewen laughed and Moira smiled to herself to see her brother so happy.

'Although he shares my disquiet about this plan,' she thought, 'he has accepted our fate willingly for the good of the estate and so should I.'

"Good morning."

Moira spun round in her chair and there was Stuart standing in the door of the Saloon. He looked even more handsome than ever.

'I must look upon him as no more than a friend,' she resolved with determination.

"I see you are eating kippers for breakfast – a good choice. I have them brought down from Arbroath especially. It is my one luxury."

Stuart put three kippers onto his plate.

He looked at Moira and hesitated before sitting down next to Ewen. It was as if he sensed Moira's wish for distance.

"Will we make good time to Tilbury, Kelpie?"

"If the weather stays like this, aye, we will be there by Tuesday morning. Did I mention that we are stopping at Queensferry to pick up another passenger?"

Moira felt most uneasy.

Another passenger?

"No, you didn't," replied Ewen, spreading strawberry jam on his bread.

"A most hearty fellow whom I met on one of my visits to Edinburgh. He lives in Morningside and is a banker I believe. He has business in London and prefers the open sea to a stuffy train. He will provide amusing company."

'The gentleman must be of good standing if he lives in Morningside,' mused Moira.

Stuart finished his kippers, rose and bowed to Moira.

"If you will excuse me, I have business to attend to on the bridge. I am afraid I do not have the luxury of long breakfasts, but please, do take your time."

He smiled as he left the Saloon.

"Hmm, this is an interesting turn of events," commented Ewen, "this fellow may be able to provide an entry into a different social circle. The Cunninghams may move in glittering circles, but a banker may have dealings with a different kind of wealth. Moira, we need as many introductions as possible."

"I agree, he may well be of some use to us. We shall resolve to make friends with him, shall we not?"

As they finished breakfast, Moira began to plot.

'A rich banker! Now he would make a fine husband. If this man is as young and handsome as Stuart, then I would not find it too much of a hardship to wed him.'

*

Later that afternoon the *Victorious* entered the Firth of Forth.

Moira stood on the deck as they passed the familiar beaches where she had walked in happier times.

As they approached Queensferry, Ewen came to stand by her side.

As Moira gazed over the great river, the wind blowing strands of her hair loose, she suddenly shivered violently. It was more than just the fresh breeze – it was as if a shadow was passing over her.

'Why do I have such a feeling of foreboding?' she thought to herself. 'I have no reason to dread the next leg of our journey.'

The *Victorious* edged towards the jetty and as the shouts of the crew rang out, the ship shuddered to a halt.

"Maybe I will have time for a wee dram," piped up Ewen, "I think I shall go and find Kelpie to see if I cannot jump ship for a while."

Moira smiled to herself. Her brother was a true Scotsman when it came to his love of their national drink.

Ten minutes later, she saw him run gleefully down the gangway like a schoolboy.

Stuart stood at the prow of the ship examining a map.

Moira walked over to him.

"Are you not joining my brother?"

Stuart's blue eyes crinkled into a smile and Moira could not prevent her heart from missing a beat.

"I do not share your brother's taste for whisky. A modest glass of ale with my dinner is my only vice."

"A temperate man is one to be valued," parried Moira gaily, pushing a strand of hair out of her eyes.

She could not believe that she had been so bold as to make such a remark.

'But I must practice before I reach London,' she thought, 'where the gentlemen will be used to forward ladies, well practised in the subtle art of flirtation.'

"Ah, here is our new passenger," said Stuart.

Walking along the narrow path that led to the jetty, Moira could see a slight figure in a dark cloak and hat walking towards them.

Moira took in his thin face and thick sideburns. The man's nose was large, almost too large for his face and his complexion ruddy. As he drew closer, she could detect the odour of cigars and strong drink.

"Lady Moira, this is Angus MacKinnon. Angus, Lady Moira Strathcarron and her brother, Lord Ewen, are fellow passengers on our journey South."

Angus MacKinnon's eyes raked over Moira from head to toe, undressing her as he took in every detail. Moira felt quite sick as she flushed under his gaze.

"Delighted to meet you."

Angus spoke in the refined tones of Morningside that were so familiar to her, but she did not care at all for his manner. In fact, she took an instant dislike to the unctuous fellow. She thought his stare lascivious and not at all polite or respectful.

'This is one fellow I must not encourage. I shall have to strike him off my list of potential husbands immediately.'

Angus was, however, not deterred by Moira's cool demeanour.

"I can see that I shall enjoy the journey all the more in your fine company, Lady Moira," began Angus, moving a little nearer to her.

Moira shuddered and stepped away from him. She fervently wished that her brother would make haste back to the ship.

"Ah, there is Ewen." Stuart was beaming as Ewen sprang up the gangway.

"Ewen, I would like you to meet your fellow passenger, Angus MacKinnon."

Ewen grasped Angus's outstretched hand and shook it warmly. Moira could tell by his flushed countenance that he had indeed availed himself of the hospitality of a local tavern, if not two.

The two men were now talking together animatedly. It appeared that they had an acquaintance in common from Stirling.

"You must pay us a visit at Lednock Castle next time you're in those parts," Ewen was saying, much to Moira's horror. "Loch Earn is only a few hours by coach away from Stirling. Father's lawyer is in Stirling – do you ken William Clooney?"

"Yes, I do," replied Angus, still casting lecherous looks in Moira's direction.

'Why does Ewen not reprimand him for looking at me in such a disrespectful manner?' thought Moira, angrily. 'He does not notice as he is seeing everything through the bottom of a whisky glass.'

"I hope you will do me the honour of sitting next to me at dinner."

Moira realised with a start that Angus was addressing her. She had been so lost in her thoughts that she had not been paying attention to the conversation.

"With so few guests for dinner, we will all be sitting next to each other," she answered, coldly.

But in spite of her chilly demeanour, Angus seemed quite undeterred. He continued to pay her compliments of the kind that she found most unwelcome.

"You are a fine looking woman, Lady Moira," said Angus, as they proceeded along the deck to the Saloon where Stuart had invited them all to take tea together.

The daylight had now faded and through the Saloon window, Moira could see the moon starting to rise in the sky.

They all chatted together for a while and drank tea and then Stuart announced that he must return to the bridge as the crew was ready to set sail.

"I am afraid that I will not be joining you for dinner tonight," he added as he was about to leave. "We will be sailing through dangerous waters and I am required on the bridge as I know the way very well. But please, do enjoy dinner."

Moira felt terribly disappointed – dining with Stuart would be the highlight of her day and she did not wish to have this awful MacKinnon fellow to spoil her meal.

As she had anticipated dinner was a strain. Angus talked animatedly all through the meal and she quite lost her appetite, pushing the roast beef around her plate in a disinterested fashion.

After the meal was finished, she quickly excused herself,

"I do apologise but I am quite tired out. I think I shall retire to my cabin."

"I will see you to your door," offered Ewen, rising from the table.

As they walked towards her cabin, Moira asked Ewen what he thought of their new passenger.

"He seems a decent fellow," replied Ewen, much to her horror. "He has invited me to play cards with him and to partake in a bottle of single Islay malt."

"Ewen, I do not care for him at all. He is I cannot describe what makes me feel so uneasy about him, but I would not trust him."

"You are tired, Moira, and don't worry, I do not intend to get drunk tonight. I have had enough for one day."

He kissed his sister on the cheek and made his way back up on deck.

Moira could hear laughter quite late into the night. She tossed and turned and finally fell into a fitful sleep.

Around midnight, she awoke with a start, her heart beating wildly – there was someone banging on her cabin door!

She hesitated before getting up – if it was Ewen, he would have called out by now and identified himself. And Stuart would not be so ungentlemanly as to knock on her door at this late hour. It was quite clear that there was no emergency and it could only be one other person – Angus MacKinnon.

Moira lay on the bed, her heart in her mouth as the knocking became persistent.

'Should I open the door or shall I ignore it?' she considered. 'If the ship is sinking, then the alarms would have sounded.'

Even so, she felt sick to her stomach. It could only be Angus.

Finally, after knocking for nearly ten minutes, she heard footsteps die away down the corridor.

'Thank Heavens his cabin is at the other end of the ship,' she sighed to herself as she moistened a handkerchief to mop her forehead. Her heart was beating so wildly she feared that she might faint.

'I shall tell Ewen tomorrow that his new friend is not to be encouraged.'

*

Because of her ordeal, Moira slept until well after nine. She awoke with a start, hearing nine bells clanging from the bridge.

She dressed hastily knowing that she would have missed Stuart for breakfast, as it was his habit to eat his early.

As she hurried towards the Saloon she could see Ewen coming towards her. His face was the colour of ash and he looked a little sick to say the least.

"Good morning, Moira," he called holding his head. "I fear I could not stomach breakfast this morning. I was up late playing cards with Angus. A fine fellow indeed."

Moira could not believe her ears – a fine fellow?

'Shall I tell him what happened last night?' she wondered before deciding that Ewen was not in a fit state. 'I will tell him later when he is feeling better.'

"Now, I am off to lie down a wee while. Will I see you later?"

"Yes, Ewen," Moira stroked her brother's brow. It was clammy and burning.

"You must drink plenty of liquid it will flush out the impurities."

"Aye," he muttered still holding his head. "I may have to take a powder."

Moira entered the Saloon to find it quite deserted. The usual fine spread lay upon the buffet table and there were hot rolls and coffee.

But her peace was soon shattered. For no sooner had she begun to eat her eggs than in walked Angus, grinning superciliously at her.

"Ah, good morning, my dear."

Moira recoiled in horror.

How dare he address her in such a familiar manner? She suddenly wished that she had already finished her meal and could excuse herself.

'I cannot bring myself to speak to him,' she thought, so she simply nodded.

His appearance had quite made her lose her appetite and she lost interest in her plate of eggs.

"I came calling last night to speak to you, but you did not answer the door," he began and then seeing her look of horror, started to laugh.

"I was only being friendly, Lady Moira."

Moira could bear it no longer. She stood up from the table and was about to run from the room, when Ewen walked in unexpectedly.

"Finished so soon?" he asked, as she ran past him.

"I fear your sister is unwell this morning," smirked Angus. "I do believe that she did not sleep well last night."

"She was not the only one," answered Ewen, "my throat is near parched."

Meanwhile, Moira was standing outside overhearing the conversation.

'The impertinence of the man,' she fumed, as she heard him explain away her sudden disappearance.

She debated if she should tell Ewen what had happened, but perhaps he would think that she had encouraged the man. She went over and over in her head every detail from the first moment they were introduced but try as she might, she could not find any evidence of having shown any signs of interest in him quite the contrary.

Even so, she decided not to inform Ewen, as she did not want to cast a pall on their voyage.

'I must resolve to be more wary around that man,' she decided, as she made her way to the safety of her cabin.

*

But she could not stay there all day the sun was shining brilliantly outside and she soon became in need of some fresh air.

'I refuse to hide like a trapped fox in a hole,' she told herself firmly, as she picked up her cloak and wound it around her. It was cold outside even though fine and the North Sea breeze was a real bone-chiller.

Up on deck, Moira enjoyed the salt spray in her face and the strong air. She paced up and down the deck awhile before noticing that Stuart was on the bridge.

'I have a fancy for some decent company,' she thought rebelliously, 'and there is no harm in mere conversation.'

Stuart bowed as Moira entered the bridge.

"Why, this is a pleasant surprise, Lady Moira," he said, smiling at her.

"I feel the need of some company. Would I be disturbing you if I stayed?"

"Of course not. We have passed the most dangerous part of the coast now and it should be easy from here. At least until we reach the Wash."

Moira noticed that Stuart was holding a book on botany. He held it close to his chest as if seeking to hide it.

"I have read that same book myself," said Moira, pointing to the tome, "most fascinating. Some of the Indochinese plants are wonderful so exotic."

Now it was Stuart's turn to blush. He looked flustered and then placed the book down on a nearby ledge.

"I studied botany at Stirling University," he confessed. "I have always been interested in flora and fauna – thus why I made for your vegetable garden the day we first met. I was destined for a career travelling the Far East to collect specimens for the Botanical Gardens in Glasgow and then I caught the sailing bug. I confess that, like so many young men, the call of the sea proved stronger."

"But surely you could have combined the two?" enquired Moira, intrigued.

"Sadly, botany is a rich man's hobby and I do not have the means."

Moira winced – she did not need reminding of his lack of finance as it was all that stood between him and the altar as far as she was concerned.

They talked at length on the subject until Moira felt she should take her leave.

"I am distracting you," she said, as he protested, "and I have some needlework in my cabin that I need to finish."

"Very well, but I have thoroughly enjoyed our talk. Nevertheless, I would ask you one favour."

"Of course," replied Moira, intrigued further.

Once again she was astonished to see Stuart blush.

"I would ask that you do not discuss my little vice with your brother or Angus. They would not deem it manly."

Moira wanted to rush over to him and kiss his full red lips. Her heart was overflowing with tenderness, in spite of her resolution to the contrary.

'If only Stuart was rich,' she thought sadly as she left the bridge. She cast one longing look backwards and then steeled herself. 'No, I must be firm. I must expunge any feelings I have for him and treat him as I would a brother.'

Hurriedly she walked along the deck with her head bent against the wind. It had changed direction and was blowing hard enough to make walking difficult.

The ship began to roll heavily and as she stumbled along, she lost her footing and fell straight into a man who was standing nearby.

She smelt whisky and tobacco and immediately assumed she had landed on Ewen.

Suddenly Moira realised in horror that it was Angus MacKinnon.

As she fell, he grabbed hold of her and refused to let her go.

"Not so proud now, Lady Moira," he snarled, pressing her close to him.

"Let me go," she pleaded.

"There is a word for women like you – you are nothing but a tease!"

Moira recoiled from his foul breath. Even though he was barely an inch taller than her, he was incredibly strong for his size. His mouth was just inches away from hers, as Moira tried to twist her head away.

"You flirted with me at dinner and gave me the impression that you would welcome a visit from me later in the evening," he snorted, his eyes bulging.

"I did nothing of the sort," asserted Moira, wriggling free at last. "You are twisted beyond words if you think that my curtness was an invitation to disturb me in a most ungentlemanly fashion."

Angus's eyes narrowed and he made as if to lunge at her.

Just then, one of the crewmen appeared at Moira's side.

"My Lady, are you all right?" he asked, the wind blowing so hard she could barely make out what he was saying to her.

"Yes, *yes*," she replied, thankful that someone had come to her aid.

"Begging your pardon, my Lady, but your brother wishes to see you below decks. He has been seasick and wishes you to go to him."

"Will you please accompany me?" Moira asked him, nervously.

The sailor had quickly got the measure of what was happening and nodded, gently taking Moira by the arm.

"Aye, gladly, my Lady."

As she turned around to leave, she could have sworn that she heard Angus saying something, his hissing voice swept away by the wind.

"I have not finished with you yet, Moira!"

Shaking, Moira was glad of the burly sailor's company to her brother's cabin where she found Ewen lying on his bunk, pale and wan.

"Well, this is a fine thing. My wee sister has found her sea legs while her big brother lies in bed like a sickly bairn."

"Ewen, there is something I must tell you."

Her brother looked closely at her pale face and realised that something untoward had happened.

"What is it? Have you been ill too?"

"No, Ewen, it is MacKinnon. He has paid unwelcome attention to me – and then became violent when I tried to fend him off."

"Are you sure you didn't misunderstand him, Moira? I cannot believe that he would show you such little respect."

Moira pulled back her cloak and pushed up the sleeve of her bodice. There on her arm was a clear set of handprints, still angry and smarting.

Ewen stared in horror.

"He – did – this?"

She could not help herself as tears sprang into her eyes.

"Yes, he did. And he threatened me that worse was to follow. Ewen, I do not understand what I have done. I have not encouraged the man, I swear it."

"Ill or not, I cannot allow my sister to be compromised. We will go straight away to Kelpie and inform him."

"Ewen, I don't want you to make a fuss if you are not well enough – "

He pulled back the covers determinedly and got up.

"It's strange. He seemed such a decent fellow too," he commented, as they made their way above deck. "I was deceived and I don't like to be made to look a fool."

Within minutes, Ewen was on the bridge telling Stuart everything about their fellow traveller's shocking behaviour.

Stuart listened and then grew silent. He called to the second mate and ordered him to turn the ship around and make for Lowestoft.

"Why are we heading there?" asked Moira, trembling.

"I will not have a seducer aboard my ship," Stuart replied quietly, yet full of simmering rage. "If the sister of my friend is not safe from this man's unwelcome attentions, then it is my duty to eject him at the earliest opportunity."

"But we are going off course," she protested.

Stuart looked deep into her eyes – his expression intense and full of quiet fire.

"I do not care if it means that you can sleep safe in your cabin. No, the man has committed a gross impropriety – he must leave as soon as we reach shore."

Moira and Ewen took their leave and retired to the Saloon.

"Well, I did not expect Stuart to react so," she exclaimed.

"It does not surprise me as he is a man of principle. His sister was ravished by an unscrupulous rogue and he hates male aggression in any form."

"I am most grateful to him. I had not expected him to take such prompt action."

"He is fond of you, Moira. But don't go getting any silly, romantic ideas about him. He hasn't two farthings to his name."

Ewen looked sternly at his sister as she turned away.

"I am quite mindful of our mission, brother."

'He must have said something to Ewen about me,' she thought joyously and then checked herself immediately. 'But I must not dwell on it. Stuart regards me as a sister. Of that I have no doubt.'

*

True to his word, Stuart had Angus MacKinnon ejected the moment they reached Lowestoft. The crew threw his suitcase off the gangway onto the quayside below.

Stuart ordered the ship to make sail straight away as the tide was still favourable.

Later that evening before dinner, he called Moira to the Saloon.

She found him, standing erect, his face shining and dressed in his kilt.

"Lady Moira," he started, as soon as she set foot inside the room, "I cannot apologise enough. Can you forgive me for being such a poor judge of character? I had no idea that Angus would turn out to be such a cad."

"Please, you must not take responsibility for another's actions. He was not an honourable man around women, but you were not to know that."

"Aye, he deceived us all and I cannot forgive him. I trust you have recovered from your ordeal?"

"Yes. A few bruises but no more. I was fortunate that one of your crew happened upon us when he did."

"Wattie did say that he thought that you were in danger. A most timely intervention – "

"I cannot thank you enough for taking such prompt action."

Moira could not breathe for her heart was beating so hard.

'He is *so* handsome and *so* kind,' she thought, looking at his face intently.

How her heart was racing. And did she imagine it or was Stuart looking at her with different eyes? Maybe the eyes of love –

They talked for quite some time. Moira was not aware of how late it was until she heard the cabin crew bringing in the evening meal.

"I trust you feel well enough to have some dinner?" asked Stuart, getting up.

"Of course, but I must go and change."

"Nonsense, you are well dressed enough."

"I wish to get rid of the stench of Mr. MacKinnon," she replied quietly, "if you will excuse me, I promise I shall not delay you."

'I do not want this voyage to end,' she said to herself, as she hurriedly tried to find her apricot chiffon dress that was meant for the London parties. 'How I wish we could sail off around the world together for ever. I would be so happy.'

But as she tidied her hair, she knew that it could never be.

CHAPTER SIX

All too soon the ship docked at Tilbury. It was already dark as they turned into the Thames Estuary. Moira stood on deck, her luggage at her side, waiting for Ewen.

"I trust that the carriage you have ordered will be waiting – "

Moira turned around to find Stuart standing behind her, silhouetted against the lights of the bridge.

"Yes, I am sure it will. Ewen does not forget the details."

"Unlike myself, I am afraid," said Stuart smiling, "I find to commit anything to memory takes the very devil of an effort."

Moira smiled. She could not see that Stuart possessed any faults – in her eyes, he was perfect.

"Will I see you on the return journey?" asked Stuart, "Ewen did not say when that might be."

"Our stay is indefinite. We have some family business to attend to and we cannot return until it is completed," replied Moira, sadly.

"You will permit me to write to you, I hope?" he enquired eagerly.

"Of course, I would be very pleased to hear from you. You know where we are staying?"

"With Lord and Lady – "

Moira laughed as he struggled to remember their name – Stuart did indeed have a poor memory.

"Cunningham. They live in Curzon Street, Mayfair."

"Now, I must take to the bridge as we dock. I shall say goodbye and hope to see you again presently. It has been most enjoyable."

Stuart bowed low and smiled. Moira could feel her heartstrings being tugged – she did not want to leave the *Victorious*.

"I am sorry to have kept you waiting, sister," Ewen's voice rang out along the deck. "Have you enjoyed the voyage – that incident with MacKinnon notwithstanding?"

"Yes, I have. I did not think that sea travel would suit me so much."

Ewen did not answer but became lost in thought. Was he dreading the end of their journey as well?

"Tilbury!" he called, pointing to the docks that now loomed in front of them.

The *Victorious* edged towards its moorings and then came the inevitable engine shut down. It was with a very heavy heart that Moira walked down the gangway to the quayside. She did not permit herself the indulgence of a backwards glance.

True to Ewen's word, the carriage was ready and waiting.

Climbing in, Moira could feel tears beginning to prick her eyes. She swallowed hard and hurriedly took her seat.

Very soon, they were on their way to Mayfair and the Cunninghams.

*

It was gone eleven o'clock when the carriage finally drew up outside the house in Curzon Street. Moira gazed up at the tall white façade and thought how small the house seemed compared to the generous proportions of most Scottish houses.

"But it looks like a doll's house," she exclaimed, "I cannot believe this is the residence of such notable people."

"Aye, and they don't have the size of house we are accustomed to seeing in Edinburgh or Glasgow. "It will be Georgian judging by its aspect. Tall and narrow."

"Since when did my brother become an expert in architecture?"

"Father told me," said Ewen. "He is knowledgeable on many subjects, not just farming and horse husbandry."

Moira felt sad at the thought of her father. He had seemed so listless, so unlike himself when they had said goodbye. It strengthened her resolve to make a good match in order to save the estate. That would make her father his old self surely.

The Cunninghams had been in bed for quite some time, but their butler, a solemn-faced man named Berbridge, was waiting to let to them in.

The slim façade of the house belied its internal extent. Stepping into the hall, they found themselves greeted by a magnificent staircase hung with a crystal chandelier.

Moira's bedroom was next to Ewen's and Berbridge indicated that Lord and Lady Cunningham's rooms were on the first floor behind the drawing room.

She quickly undressed by gaslight and then slipped in between the fine linen sheets. The fire in the grate glowed warmly but the room was still quite cold.

She sank deep into the feather mattress and almost instantly fell asleep.

The next morning, Moira was woken by a maid bringing in a tray of tea.

"Her Ladyship breakfasts at nine, my Lady, and would be pleased if you would join her," said the maid, as she rekindled the fire. She soon had it roaring away.

Moira pulled out a blue plaid dress that she deemed suitable and dressed quickly.

As the hall clock struck nine, she found her way downstairs and was directed by Berbridge into the dining room. Lady Cunningham was waiting for her.

"Dearest Moira, how pleased I am to see you. And looking so well."

She clasped Moira's hand warmly and kissed her on the cheek. Although the Cunninghams were very well to do, Lady Cunningham was refreshingly informal.

"And is your handsome brother well?"

"I am sure he will be down presently, Lady Cunningham."

"My dear, please call me Sarah. I do so want us to be as sisters whilst you are here. There is no need for stiff titles in this house – you are amongst friends."

"Thank you so much."

Moira took her place at the table and immediately was given a plate of eggs and kedgeree by Berbridge. Another servant poured her tea into a fine bone china cup.

Lady Cunningham began to chatter excitedly.

"My dear, I cannot tell you how many invitations have been arriving. The Season is well and truly upon us and simply everyone who is anyone is entertaining. I do hope you are well rested, as you will need all your strength to dance. The first party is tonight at the Duke of Aberfair's house in Hanover Square. It is quite near here."

"Indeed?" replied Moira, slightly nervous.

She had not thought she would be plunged into the social whirl quite so rapidly.

"Good morning to you all."

Ewen stood in the doorway, now fully recovered from his arduous journey.

Lady Cunningham rose and kissed him on the cheek he was quite taken aback by her forward manner and did not know how to respond.

"Sit down, do. Berbridge will bring you eggs, bacon, kedgeree whatever you wish."

"Aye, I am quite hungry, thank you," responded Ewen, his eyes shining with delight. It was hard not to show pleasure after many months of deprivation at Lednock.

"I was just telling your sister that there is a coming-out party for the Duke of Aberfair's youngest daughter tonight."

"Grand," commented Ewen, tucking into an enormous plate of food.

"If you are in the mood for seeking a bride, there will be plenty of eligible young ladies present," added Lady Cunningham, mischievously.

Moira giggled to herself, any concerns she had about lack of available partners were vanishing.

"Now, what will you do with yourselves until then?"

"I had thought maybe a walk around Hyde Park – I so long to see it. Ewen, will you accompany me?"

"Mmm," he nodded, his mouth full.

"Please take my carriage, if you wish. I have household business this morning so I am afraid I cannot come with you. Luncheon will be at half-past twelve, so be sure to be back in time."

She rose and left the dining room.

"How did you sleep?" enquired Ewen, sitting back in his chair, pleasantly full.

"Like a baby. And you?"

"Aye, the same. Now, let us take the morning air, I have a mind to see some sights."

And so, some twenty minutes later, the two of them found themselves in a carriage bound for Hyde Park. Moira pulled a woollen rug over her legs and snuggled up to Ewen against the chill of the morning.

"It sounds as if this party could provide plenty of interesting introductions."

Moira smiled as they rounded the Serpentine with its ducks and geese.

"Aye, and I am certain that you will have no trouble attracting attention."

Moira looked away, she wished she could be as sure as her brother – she was still convinced that she would forever be in the shade of the fashionable London ladies.

As the carriage continued its way around the park, Moira began to wonder if Stuart would indeed honour his promise of writing to her.

'I hope he remembers where we are staying he did seem rather vague.'

But she did not have time to think too much about Stuart as day passed in a flash.

After a fine luncheon, Lady Cunningham took her to William Whitley's emporium in Queensway and bought her some new Nottingham lace handkerchiefs.

Moira was enchanted by the fantastic department store, with its many floors of merchandise. As she ascended the central marble staircase, she felt that she had stepped into a dream world.

She gazed longingly at the ball gowns made of tulle and silk, all in the latest styles. She thought with a sinking heart of her favourite apricot chiffon that looked so out of date with its wrongly shaped skirt. These gowns had small neat pads at the back instead of a bustle and the bodices were so much more tailored.

Exhausted, she flopped into the waiting carriage and dozed all the way back.

All too soon, it was time to leave for the ball. Moira regarded herself in the cheval mirror in her bedroom and groaned. Although her diamonds gave her an expensive look, her dress ruined the effect.

'I wonder if Sarah has a dress she could lend me, we are around the same size – '

But pride would not allow her ask such a favour. And it might lead to Lady Cunningham wondering about the Strathcarrons' finances. Moira hoped that living in an unfashionable part of the country would be sufficient to explain away her hideously out-of-date dress.

"My dear, you look exquisite," gushed Lady Cunningham as Moira descended the stairs. "I have a mink wrap that will set off the colour of your dress perfectly."

Moira was not too proud to accept Lady Cunningham's generous attempt at smartening her up and she gratefully accepted the proffered wrap.

"Splendid. Now come, both of you, the carriage awaits."

Ten minutes later, the Cunninghams' carriage pulled up outside a very grand residence in Hanover Square. There were already a number of similar conveyances lining the street, each disgorging their glittering contents.

'Everyone looks so glamorous,' moaned Moira to herself.

She had spotted a young girl around her age in a pale lemon dress and gamboge coloured, velvet cloak entering the Aberfair's home. She wore fresh flowers in her hair and her gown was trimmed with tiny beads. As she turned, Moira could see the narrow bustle sitting beautifully behind her.

'So fashionable. My skirts are all wrong. My bustle is *too* big.'

Ewen's eyes were bulging with delight.

"Aye, the lassies are bonny in London," he exclaimed, watching the girl in the lemon gown. An identically dressed girl, who was obviously her sister accompanied her.

The two girls were laughing gaily as they disappeared into the hallway.

By the time that Moira was helped from the carriage by the Cunninghams' driver, she was shaking with nerves. Lady Cunningham took hold of her arm to steady her.

"Do not worry, my dear. You look as charming as any present tonight."

Moira smiled gratefully at her – Lady Cunningham was so kind.

The Aberfair's house was immaculate, the furnishings rich and of the best possible quality. Moira and Ewen gawped in wonder at an enormous French chandelier.

Everywhere seemed to sparkle – from the crystal glasses full of champagne to the Venetian glass gas-lamp shades. There were six-branched candelabra in the dining room and everywhere they looked there was silverware of the kind that the Strathcarrons had once owned but had since discreetly disappeared.

Moira tried hard not to seem overly impressed, as she knew that this would mark her out as a provincial. She *was* an Earl's daughter and could hold her head up as such.

Almost as soon as they arrived, Lady Cunningham was taken to the Duke.

"Come, both of you," she beckoned, as a footman led her to where the Aberfairs were holding court.

Moira followed her tentatively with Ewen close at her heels. Everyone they passed seemed so elegant. She felt sure that dozens of pairs of critical eyes were appraising her.

"You look a picture, sister," whispered Ewen. "I have noticed many young men looking your way."

"Ah, Lady Cunningham. How wonderful to see you and looking so well."

The Duke of Aberfair was a small man with white hair and a distinguished countenance. His bright blue eyes sparkled with mischief.

Moira could detect a slight Welsh accent and this made her warm to him.

"And these are my dear friends, Lord and Lady Strathcarron. They are Scott, the Earl of Strathcarron's children."

The Duke took Moira's hand and kissed it, before greeting Ewen warmly.

"Delighted, delighted! How is Scott? I have not had the pleasure of seeing him for quite some time – "

"Father has been a little unwell of late," spoke up Moira.

"I am sorry to hear that, I trust it is nothing serious?"

"No, just a lingering cold that will not abate."

The Duke spoke a while with Ewen on the subject of horses, before turning to introduce his daughter who was standing with a group of friends.

Almost immediately there was a burst of girlish laughter and Ewen disappeared in amongst the group. Moira could see the girls flashing their eyes at him and fanning themselves coquettishly.

'And it is hardly warm enough for that,' she thought, almost jealous that her brother had been such an instant success.

Lady Cunningham took her around the room, introducing her to various people. They all seemed so grand.

As the evening wore on, Moira saw very little of Ewen. Whenever she looked for him, he was surrounded by girls, all making him 'talk Scottish', as they put it.

She could see that he was enjoying himself.

"Moira, there is a young gentleman who wishes to meet you."

Lady Cunningham had returned with a thin-looking fellow in a sober suit.

"This is Charles, his father is the Bishop of Westminster."

"Delighted to meet you," replied Moira, casting a discerning eye over the young man and immediately comparing him with Stuart. She found him somewhat lacking.

"Lady Cunningham tells me that you are Scottish. I am fond of that land myself hill walking is a hobby of mine."

"There are plenty of hills to climb around Loch Earn," answered Moira politely.

"I have walked the entire length of Hadrian's Wall," continued Charles, not listening to Moira at all. "It was a most bracing experience."

Moira could feel her eyelids drooping as he told her, in great detail, about each and every walk he had undertaken in the last year.

'How I wish Stuart was here,' she thought. 'He would not chatter on at me endlessly I wonder if he *will* write to me?'

As soon as she could politely withdraw from Charles's boring company, Moira excused herself.

Walking around the house, she could not stop from feeling very much like the poor relation. The girls all seemed so confident and at ease while the men paid them fulsome compliments.

Not a single gentleman apart from Ewen had passed comment on her appearance.

The party dragged on endlessly and Moira was heartily relieved when Lady Cunningham appeared to inform her that their carriage was ready to leave.

"So soon," exclaimed Ewen.

"You will have plenty of chance to see those young ladies again at the Earl of Hackfield's masked ball tomorrow night," remarked Lady Cunningham, as they departed.

Moira remained silent all the way back to Curzon Street – all she could think of was Stuart Weston –.

*

The next morning, Lady Cunningham whisked Moira off to Bond Street for some shopping before the next social event.

"The cream of London Society will be present," she twittered, as they strode along the famous street full of enticing shops. "I am sure that both my Scottish visitors will be a raging success."

"If last night is anything to go by, then I am sure that Ewen will acquire many admirers," replied Moira, feeling quite depressed. Not even the finery displayed in the shops could raise her spirits.

Later Moira found herself with Ewen back in Lady Cunningham's carriage on their way to Hampstead.

The Earl's house was on the edge of the Heath. Moira instantly took a liking to its aspect and the surrounding area – the hilly greenery was most unexpected in the middle of London.

"Now you must wear your masks," ordered Lady Cunningham, as the carriage pulled up. "Remember, you cannot take them off until midnight."

Once inside Moira was greeted with an opulence that far outstripped that of the Duke of Aberfair's house.

There were so many servants that it made her quite envious.

"Ah, Lady Cunningham, so these are your Highland friends."

It was the Countess of Hackfield. She was wearing a navy silk dress embroidered with jet beads. On her head was a magnificent diamond tiara. Her mask was an understated affair, but Moira guessed that it was authentically Venetian by its style.

Within minutes, the Countess had led Ewen away to a trio of young ladies who were standing nearby.

Moira watched as, once more, Ewen was fawned over and spoiled.

'Ah, watching Ewen gives me very little amusement. I will take a turn around the house.'

It was easy for Moira to lose herself in the thronging crowd.

After a while, she became quite tired and sought out a quiet corner. Finding herself in the conservatory, she slipped out of the glass doors and into the garden.

All around the garden were masses of Chinese lanterns, which swung gently in the breeze. Moira thought the effect most charming.

She was standing near the fountain, enjoying the sight of the water splashing from the mouth of a stone dolphin, when she became suddenly aware that she was not alone.

Turning towards the knot garden, she saw a man in a highwayman's mask standing quite close by.

"Oh, you startled me!" she cried, clutching her throat.

"You do not care for crowds either?" the man enquired.

Moira noted that he had not apologised for surprising her and became wary.

"I simply wanted to see the gardens."

The man drew closer – she could not see his eyes behind the mask.

"There is little to see in the darkness – " he replied, almost sinisterly.

It was something in the way that the man spoke that was familiar to Moira. She racked her brains. That voice, she had surely heard it before, but where?

"I do not mind the darkness," she said lightly.

"Then you are a brave young lady – there are plenty inside who would not dare to venture out. The gardens back onto the heath and there are wild animals roaming."

"Where I come from, we are used to them. They hold no fear for me."

"Such brave talk. But I'll warrant that you are not always so doughty."

Moira hesitated.

There was something in the man's manner that was almost threatening. She did not care for the direction the conversation was leading.

"I am sure I do not know to what you allude. With respect, you are a stranger and ill placed to make comment on my constitution, I feel."

The man laughed a hollow menacing laugh.

It made Moira's blood run cold.

'But I have heard that laughter before,' she thought, frantically searching her memory.

"You do not remember where we last met, do you, Lady Moira?"

In that moment, Moira felt utter panic.

Who was this man and why was he being so threatening? Her heart began to race as she looked towards the lights of the conservatory. The man was standing between her and her escape route.

He began to move towards her and she could smell whisky and cigarettes.

"We have, I believe, some unfinished business – "

It was then that Moira remembered who it was.

It was Angus MacKinnon!

"How how did you get here?" she stammered, trying to back away.

He did not reply, but laughed a black sinister laugh and made a lunge for her.

Moira tried to run away but Angus grabbed her skirts and dragged her towards the bushes.

"Help! Help!" she screamed, trying to push him away.

"You think you are so high and mighty, madam, but I know that you are a woman of easy virtue. I can see it in your eyes you are naught but a soiled dove!"

Moira shut her eyes and howled, as loud as her lungs would permit.

Within seconds she felt herself flung to the ground and then a woman was helping her to sit up.

"There, there, dear," she said, wafting a bottle of *sal volatile* under her nose.

"Stop that man!" came a loud male voice. "He has attacked this young lady and must be apprehended."

"Lady Moira. I cannot describe how sorry I am that we appear to have a miscreant in our midst."

It was the Countess.

She ordered a footman to help Moira up and then to take her into the library for a nip of brandy.

"Please, go, leave me," she told the footman, after he had poured her a drink. "Would you be so good as to find my brother, Lord Strathcarron. He is the young gentleman with the red hair and the *pierrot* mask."

The footman bowed and left the room.

Some fifteen minutes later, Ewen tore into the library, his mask in his hand.

"Moira, are you all right? The footman said something about an attack and a man in the garden – "

"It was MacKinnon."

"What!"

"He must have found an alternative route to London. But Heaven only knows how he knew we would be at this party. I do believe he sought to take his revenge after his unceremonious ejection from the *Victorious*."

"The blackguard!"

"My Lord, the Police have been alerted and a man has been caught running towards the Heath. He has been locked in the wine cellar until they arrive."

It was the Hackfields' butler.

"Would your Lordship like me to have your carriage made ready to leave?"

"Aye, I think that would be for the best."

"But Ewen, you are having such a good time. I do not wish to ruin your evening."

"There are to be no arguments, sister. Besides, the footman is here with our cloaks."

Lady Cunningham was most upset to hear of Moira's confrontation with Angus.

"How on earth did he procure an invitation to the Hackfields' party?" she wondered as the carriage sped away from the party "He is a banker and knows many an influential businessman in the City," said Ewen, grimacing. Since they had left he had not let go of Moira's hand.

"I can only assume that he must have connections somehow."

"Shocking! *Utterly* shocking! The Hackfields were mortified that such a character should have gained access to their circle. He will not be welcome in any good houses from now on."

The rocking motion of the carriage began to send Moira to sleep. She was totally exhausted from her awful experience and soon drifted off.

Arriving back at Curzon Street, the carriage jolted to a halt.

'It would make me so happy should I return to a letter from Stuart,' thought Moira, hopefully. She knew that here in London, there were as many as six postal deliveries a day in some areas.

And so, when Berbridge let them in, she asked if there had been any messages or letters delivered for her.

"I am afraid not, my Lady, but the first post should arrive at half-past seven tomorrow morning. Is your Ladyship waiting for a special delivery?"

She shook her head, suddenly feeling quite foolish. Why should Stuart write to her? They were not sweethearts nor even established friends.

"Moira, will you have a nightcap before you retire?" asked Lady Cunningham.

"Thank you, Sarah, but I feel I need to sleep."

She went to kiss her brother on the cheek.

"Dearest Ewen, you can tell me all your news tomorrow over breakfast. I can tell by the look in your eyes that you met someone special tonight."

Ewen blushed then bowed.

"Aye, I did. But I will save it until tomorrow. Goodnight Moira. Sleep tight."

Up in her room, Moira took off her dress and hung it over one of the many chairs in the bedroom. Her feet hurt and her slippers were ruined from the mud she had picked up in the garden.

Even her diamonds did not seem to shine so brilliantly.

Staring at her reflection in the mirror, she felt a sense of hopelessness.

'I will never attract a suitable husband whilst I look so much the Scottish simpleton. Even before that awful MacKinnon ruined my evening, I did not have as much as a sniff of a likely suitor. Perhaps it is something in my demeanour.'

The maid had removed the warming pan already and the sheets were quite cool, but still Moira was grateful to slide into bed.

The fire in the grate was burning low and she was soon drifting off.

'I must make a big effort at the next ball,' she resolved, drowsily. 'I cannot be such a dismal wet blanket any more. I must put this whole MacKinnon incident behind me and look forward. The same goes for Stuart – why, the man cannot even honour a promise. Ewen is counting on me and failure is not an option.'

She was soon fast asleep, dreaming of the Highlands and better days at Lednock Castle.

But would her dreams ever become reality?

She knew that only time would tell, but right now, the future was not looking good –

CHAPTER SEVEN

Moira was most surprised to find Ewen already seated at the dining table when she came down for breakfast the next morning.

"Good day, Moira," he called, wolfing down porridge and thickly buttered toast.

"You are in good spirits, brother. I hope you are going to tell me more of the young lady who is obviously responsible."

"Aye, I confess I am exhilarated. The young lady is called Mary Anne, she is twenty and her father is a Marquis. She is enchanting and it is my intention to call upon her this very morning."

He seemed so excited that Moira was quite touched. Her brother – *in love*!

"What does she look like? Is she pretty?"

"Very. You could not mistake her for her hair is as red as mine. I told her that she must have Scots blood."

Moira had the vaguest recollection of a rather feisty-looking girl with titian-coloured hair who was laughing very loudly all night. She had been one of the girls who had surrounded Ewen upon their arrival at the ball.

"Ah, yes, Lady Mary Anne Kirkbride," intervened Lady Cunningham, using the kind of tone of voice that Moira instantly discerned held more than a hint of disapproval. "The Marquis of Kirkbride has had a somewhat chequered past."

"But they are rich?" Ewen could not hide his anxiety.

Moira glared at her brother – it was imperative that Lady Cunningham did not gain any hint that Ewen's choice of partner was dictated by their dreadful finances.

"Terribly," was Lady Cunningham's reply.

But there was something in her reluctance to elaborate that made Moira wary.

'If Ewen proposes, then I shall have to swallow my feelings and be glad for him,' she decided, as he rose from the table. 'But surely he would not want to propose after just one meeting?'

"Moira, I will see you later. Sarah."

He bowed elegantly and left the room.

"Such a handsome young man," commented Lady Cunningham, putting down her napkin.

"Moira, dear, how are you feeling this morning after your ordeal?"

"I am perfectly fine, thank you, Sarah."

"But I do sense that perhaps you are not enjoying your stay with us as much as you could and I am most anxious to help. Do not protest. I have seen those long sad looks of yours. Tell me, is there anything I can do to help? You are worried about your father's health naturally – "

Her words had a devastating effect on Moira. She could not help herself she simply burst into tears.

Sobbing as if her heart would break, she was led into the morning room by Lady Cunningham, who shielded her from the stares of the servants.

Closing the door behind them, Lady Cunningham bade her sit on the button-backed sofa and sank down next to her.

Moira blew her nose into her new lace hanky and began,

"I really should not be telling you our private family business, Sarah, but you have been *so* kind. I feel I can trust you and I have no one else to talk to. It is my father, he is much more indisposed than I have been able to reveal."

Lady Cunningham shook her head in disbelief.

"Is the Earl in danger? Moira, you must tell me."

"We are not certain. His malady seems to be springing from a deep melancholy. The cause we know not – "

Moira winced inwardly as she told the lie.

'But I cannot tell her more, even though I long to,' she thought to herself. 'My family would be mortified if they knew I had spoken so freely and Ewen would never forgive me.'

"I trust you have sought medical advice?"

"Mother had been advised that he needed rest and that is why we decided to return your visit."

"Ah, all becomes clearer now."

Moira was relieved that she had not told her more and Lady Cunningham seemed to be satisfied with her explanation as she did not question her further.

Just then, the door to the morning room burst open and Ewen stormed in with a face like thunder.

"Ewen. We had not expected you back for hours yet."

He paced the room, speechless with rage, his eyes bulging and his complexion florid.

"I cannot believe it! Is this how fine London ladies comport themselves?"

"Ewen, please – you must calm yourself," soothed Moira in a cool voice.

"I cannot!"

"Then you must tell us what has upset you," Lady Cunningham wanted to know, ringing for Berbridge.

"Mary Anne, *the hoyden*!"

"Ewen," called Moira, shocked. "Please refrain from using such language."

"Begging your pardon, sister – Sarah."

Berbridge knocked and upon being bidden to enter, slid quietly into the room.

"Some coffee, please, Berbridge."

Lady Cunningham knew just what to do in such circumstances. Lord Cunningham who had taken himself off to the shires to hunt was prone to foul tempers.

"Och, I am sorry," apologised Ewen, sitting down on the sofa next to Moira, "but I have just made a fool of myself."

"How so?"

"I called upon Mary Anne and when I arrived, I was made to sit in the hallway like a servant, along with a line of other young men, who had also come to call on her."

Moira was not at all surprised.

"The young lady in question was out shopping. Can you believe it? And when she came back, she inspected us as if we were a line of stud cattle!"

Lady Cunningham's eyebrows shot up into her hairline – she was not used to such plain speaking.

"Of course, I was not going to bear being treated like that and so I left."

Looking at his sister, he suddenly realised that she had been crying. Her nose was a most unattractive shade of red, as were her eyes.

"But steady. Here I am, prattling on like an old woman when it is plain that something has upset you. Pray, what is it, sister? I hope that it's not MacKinnon again?"

"It is just a little homesickness. Ah, look, here is the coffee. Thank you, Sarah."

Lady Cunningham waited until Berbridge had poured the coffee, then she moved gracefully towards the door.

Without hesitating, she took her leave and closed the door behind her.

"Now that she has gone, will you tell me what has upset you," demanded Ewen.

Moira took a deep breath.

"I wish to go home, Ewen. I hate London and it's quite clear that I will not meet a husband here. I feel I could have more luck in Glasgow."

"But you cannot go alone. That would be scandalous," replied Ewen, getting up and pacing the floor. "You must remember why we came here, sister, and mind your duty. We have to do something to help father regain the estate and neither your happiness nor mine comes into it. Do you understand?"

Moira was quite shocked at his tone but she knew he was right.

"Oh, I am being such a selfish girl," she cried, throwing herself into her brother's arms. "I must confess to feeling a little jealous of your success – even if things did not go well with Mary Anne. There are so many fine young ladies in London who find you fascinating. It is only a matter of time before you find the right one."

"And you will meet a suitable young man," soothed Ewen. "I know it."

'I wish I could believe him – ' thought Moira, 'but in my heart, I do not think that I will meet anyone I like as much as I do Stuart Weston.'

*

The next few weeks were indeed a social whirl. Lady Cunningham whisked them off to many a fine ball and, as Christmas drew closer, there were charity concerts to attend, exhibitions to visit and carol singing in Berkeley Square.

Moira could not help but look over her shoulder at these events, fearing that Angus MacKinnon was present. But he failed to materialise.

She met a couple of charming young men and one, the son of a judge, did call on her a few times. But interest soon fizzled out when it became clear that he did not possess the necessary financial wherewithal.

In the meantime, Ewen was becoming very much the gay young blade and there was a constant stream of letters on scented paper that found their way to Curzon Street.

"You will break so many hearts," observed Lady Cunningham, as yet another two arrived for him one fine December morning. "You are the talk of London."

Ewen blushed deeply and shuffled his feet. For all his bluster, he was still quite shy around women. However, Moira hardly recognised him from the bluff, man's man who had left Scotland only a few weeks previously.

"So many young ladies – there must be one whom you favour above all the others?" asked Moira, teasing him.

"No. I have yet to meet the pearl of my heart," shrugged Ewen. "I will know her when I see her. And you, sister, what has become of your serious young man?"

It was now Moira's turn to blush.

"He turned out to unsuitable after all," she answered, giving Ewen a meaningful look that he understood immediately.

Ewen and Moira sat down on the comfortable sofas and watched the sun streaming in through the windows of the drawing room.

"Ewen, do you think you could ever live in London?"

"No, I miss the Highlands too much already. London is all very well, but you cannot beat the air and the aspect at Loch Earn."

"Do you think we will be successful, Ewen? We have so little time left – "

"Moira, we were agreed that if we needed to stay for Christmas, then we would."

"Yes, I know, but I miss mother and I would hate not to see our parents at Christmas. It would not seem like a festive time at all if we were stuck here."

"I do understand, sister, but for all we ken, the creditors may have already begun to dismantle the estate. Was not the inventory due last week?"

"Yes, it was."

"It seems strange that we haven't had any news from home."

"Maybe, but mother will be busy with looking after father and then there is the estate to run."

"Aye, but it more or less runs itself at this time of year. It is only come lambing season in January that help would be needed."

Moira's heart sank. *January*. She was so hoping to be home for Christmas or Hogmanay at the very least.

Ewen caught her look of horror.

"Moira, we must never lose sight of why we are here. While I have every confidence that I will soon find a suitable match, *you* have to make more of an effort."

Ewen's words stung but she knew that he spoke the truth. But she found flirting so hard that when she met someone, she could not help comparing him with Stuart.

How it grieved her that he had not written. Long weeks had passed and she had stopped eagerly anticipating the post for it always brought nothing. She was so depressed by this turn of affairs that she could not even feel angry with him.

"Moira?"

"Yes, Ewen, you are right as ever. But it is so long since we had news of home. I long to hear if father is improving."

"I am sure he is as well as can be expected else mother would have sent for us."

"Sarah thinks we are here to give him a rest."

"Then it is as well that she believes it. Moira, you must not speak to her about our true reason for being here. You must promise me that."

Moira nodded her assent, but felt resentfulness growing in her heart.

'Oh, why must we find ourselves in this situation? I do so wish we had never met Larry Harwood.'

*

Later that afternoon Moira joined Lady Cunningham in her carriage.

The weather had changed and a thin mist hung over Hyde Park as they made their way to Lady Thompkin Smythe's house in Kensington.

Moira gazed up in wonderment as they passed the statue of Prince Albert in Hyde Park. Such a fine man, she thought and so devoted to the Queen.

The call was a pleasant one and Lady Thompkin-Smythe was a wonderful hostess. Her drawing room was as busy as any doctor's surgery and the poor little maid was run off her feet bringing tea and answering the door.

Afterwards, as they drove home, Lady Cunningham discreetly asked Moira if her brother might be looking for a bride during his stay.

"You are right," replied Moira. "Ewen thought it high time that he turned his attention to marriage. He has not had much success in Scotland and so thought that perhaps he would fare better in London. It is so important that he weds and produces an heir – the Strathcarrons are but a small clan and there is no other to follow him."

"That is a pity. I had thought that there were many fine Scottish ladies who might take his fancy. I am afraid that many of the young ladies in London are rather flighty as he found out with that Mary Anne creature. And you, my dear, am I right in thinking that you too are also searching?"

Moira blushed deeply and then confessed,

"That is also true. I am young, but mother is most keen for me to marry ere long. She was married by the time she was twenty and wishes me to follow suit."

"But that awful business with the MacKinnon fellow tell me, dear, what really happened?"

"You know already, Sarah. He accosted me in the Hackfields' garden and then tried to attack me – "

"I was told that you had met him before. Ewen mentioned that there had been an incident on your journey when you were on Mr. Weston's ship."

At the mention of Stuart's name, Moira's heart beat so fast that it took her breath away. She had been trying her best not to think about him, but during the long lonely hours of the night, she had longed so to hear from him.

Try as she might, Moira realised that her feelings were no longer under her control. She loved him.

Yes. She loved him!

"Dear, if it is too painful – "

Lady Cunningham's gentle voice broke into her thoughts and made her start. Moira became quite cross for allowing herself the luxury of thinking of Stuart.

"MacKinnon joined us at Queensferry and from the moment he arrived, he regarded me in an unseemly manner. He had a way of turning things round so I was made to feel like I was responsible for what happened."

"Which was?"

"He tried to force himself upon me and kiss me."

Lady Cunningham let out a gasp. She put her arm around Moira and hugged her.

"You poor, poor darling. I had no idea that it was as bad as that. I must make sure that man will never be received amongst my friends again. I shall write to everyone presently and inform them of the true nature of this – this *evil* man!"

She paused for thought and then continued,

"But you must not let one bad egg put you off looking for a husband. There are plenty of eligible young gentlemen in London Society and I will make it my business to introduce you to as many decent ones as possible. There – we have a plan."

Moira smiled thinly. Sarah was so kind almost like a mother to her. She did not wish to seem ungrateful but she did not want to meet any other young men.

Although she had not told Ewen, she was secretly pinning all her hopes on him making a sufficiently good match so that she did not have to marry for money.

'I fear that Stuart has set a standard that others will fail to reach,' she sighed.

Moira felt heavy of heart as she climbed up the steps of the Cunningham's house. Berbridge opened the door with his usual solemn expression.

"My Lady," he announced. "His Lordship has returned from the shires."

"Oh, dear," Lady Cunningham cried, turning to Moira. "And I was so hoping we could arrange some more 'at homes'. Laurence gets upset when I have more than one a week. I have tried to tell him that there is nothing wrong, but he does not agree."

"My Lady, there is a letter for you and one has come for your guests."

Berbridge bowed and presented Lady Cunningham with a silver salver.

"This has the Brampton seal. I wonder what news there is from them."

"And this is your Ladyship," Berbridge proffered the salver in Moira's direction.

For a fleeting second, her heart skipped a beat.

'Perhaps it is from Stuart.'

And then she remembered that Berbridge had said that it was for both her and Ewen. Gazing at the familiar writing, she saw that it was a letter from home.

"Thank you, I will wait until my brother returns before I open it."

"Oh, Heavens! This is awful. A calamity," exclaimed Lady Cunningham, dropping her letter to the floor.

"Sarah, what is it? Is it bad news?"

By this time, Lady Cunningham was openly weeping.

Moira picked up the letter, and then hastily took her by the arm and led her into the drawing room.

"Oh, I cannot believe it."

"Sarah, please tell me."

Sitting down on the sofa, she composed herself, dabbing her eyes.

"A dear, dear friend of mine, the Duke of Brampton, has had a dreadful accident and has been killed. His boat capsized on the Solent and all were lost. His eldest son, Louis, was also in the boat. This is terrible, terrible news."

"There were no survivors?"

"None. Oh, poor Prudence! Losing not only a husband but her son as well. There is just her and a daughter left. Dear, would you forgive me if I left you to your own devices? Laurence should know of this news immediately and I simply must put pen to paper and express my condolences."

"Of course," replied Moira, suddenly feeling quite unwell.

'What if our letter contains bad news too?' she thought. 'Oh, where is Ewen?'

At long last, she heard the sound of Ewen's voice in the hall. Ewen entered the room wearing a worried expression.

"Moira, what is the matter?"

She did not speak.

She simply held out the letter bearing the family crest.

Ewen took it from her and stared at it for an eternity.

"You did not open it?"

"No, I wanted to wait until you had returned. Just in case it was bad news."

The two of them sat looking at the letter. Finally, Ewen could bear it no longer. He picked it up from the table and ripped it open.

"Well?" demanded Moira, fearing what it might contain.

"It is from mother," he began.

"Is she well? Is father well?"

"Moderately, aye. But there is more – the American Bank has sent a representative to Lednock Castle to go over the contents of the inventory they submitted. Moira, do you ken what this means?"

Moira looked at her brother blankly.

"If they have sent a man to do a second inventory, then that means they will shortly be putting everything up for auction!"

Moira gasped and fell to her knees.

"But Ewen, they cannot just sell everything from beneath us. Surely there has to be a court hearing or something?"

"No, these people can do as they like," he replied, grimly.

"Sister, we do not have much time – a month at most. We must redouble our efforts to find wealthy spouses – it is the only way to save Lednock!"

Moira was speechless with horror.

'We have much less time than I thought to stem the tide of the inevitable,' she groaned to herself miserably.

Ewen was chewing his knuckles, his face so very pale.

"Sister, we have to make every effort to do what we set out to achieve. Parties and such are all very well, but this is no longer a game. The very future of the Strathcarrons and Lednock is at stake. Are you willing to put your all into finding a husband?"

"Yes, I will," replied Moira, turning her face away so that he could not see her tears. "Only today Sarah mentioned there were more young men for me to meet."

Ewen grunted his approval and handed Moira the letter. As she read it, her tears streaming down her cheeks, one thought kept repeating in her brain,

'Oh, Stuart. *Stuart.* Where are you when I need you?'

But deep in her heart, she knew that he could not save her from the inevitable, and that thought made her weep even more.

CHAPTER EIGHT

No sooner had Lord Cunningham greeted them than he was whisked away again. Moira and Ewen saw him but briefly before he and his wife left for Hampshire.

"My dears, I am sure you will find plenty of amusement without me," Lady Cunningham had said as she waved from her carriage. "Berbridge has the invitations for all the parties over the next few days so please, go and enjoy yourselves. I have written to everyone to tell them that I am unable to attend because of the Brampton's funerals."

As the carriage disappeared, the postman arrived bearing a whole sheaf of letters from people who were also going to the funerals and who were cancelling their parties.

"What are we going to do with ourselves now?" groaned Ewen, as he opened yet another note that stated that the writer deeply regretted the inconvenience, but felt it expedient to cancel all social engagements.

"This is terrible. How can we achieve our aim if we are unable to meet new people?"

"Here is another," said Moira. "So many people seemed to know the Duke of Brampton. London will be a ghost town for the next few days."

"And to think, Christmas is but a week and a half away, sister, and all will stop."

"But there will still be Christmas Eve balls and then New Year celebrations."

Ewen left the drawing room, huffing and puffing. It seemed that whatever Moira said would not be calm him.

'I shall let him be for a while, but without Sarah, I cannot go out and about – it is not seemly for me to be seen in public without a chaperone.'

Moira felt miserable at the prospect of being housebound for the next few days. Ewen, being a man, was able to come and go as he pleased without the kind of restraints that were placed on her as a young lady.

'I shall catch up on my reading,' Moira decided.

And so, she made herself comfortable in the morning room with her copy of *David Copperfield*. Moira did so like Mr. Dickens' novels and thought it a pity that he was no longer alive to write more.

'I wonder what he would have made of my own situation?' she muttered to herself, as she opened her book, 'truly it is the stuff of novels!'

*

The next day Ewen was feeling in a considerably better humour. He suggested to Moira that they take a trip to Fortnum and Mason's in Piccadilly for Christmas shopping.

"We should find something for Sarah," he said, ringing for Berbridge to call a Hackney carriage. "We cannot afford much, but I hear that their food hall is wonderful."

"That is an excellent idea, Ewen," agreed Moira, pleased that she now had an opportunity to leave the house.

"I will go upstairs and fetch my hat and coat."

Moira felt more cheerful as she stepped into the Hackney carriage, even though the day was dreary and cold.

Wrapping herself in the warm cashmere blankets provided by the footman, she allowed her thoughts to dwell for a while on Stuart. There had still been no letter and she had found that as the days wore on, she was thinking of him less often.

"Moira, we need to think of another plan in case this enforced mourning for the Bramptons affects the remainder of the social calendar leading up to Christmas," announced Ewen, as the carriage took off down Curzon Street.

"We can hardly just arrive at people's homes and expect them to entertain us. We still do not know anyone well enough to call upon them without Sarah," added Moira, ever mindful of the correct etiquette.

"Och! I cannot abide these silly rules," he answered, testily, "back home, if I want to visit a friend or someone in the village – I just turn up!"

"Ewen, we are in London and this is how they do things here – "

"Which is why I prefer the company of good honest farmers."

"Are you telling me that you have not enjoyed the parties and the company of the many pretty young ladies you have met?" said Moira, teasing him.

"Harumph!" coughed Ewen, gazing out of the carriage windows at a group of elegant young ladies making their way down Bond Street.

After a pleasant turn around Swan and Edgar's in Piccadilly, they felt thirsty.

"Shall we visit Fortnum and Mason's restaurant for some tea?" suggested Moira.

"Aye, grand."

Moira understood that many pretty young ladies were in the habit of taking tea there, which could have been the reason for Ewen's enthusiasm.

Inside Fortnum and Masons, there were so many lovely things that Moira became distracted and almost forgot the real reason for their visit.

"Moira, will you please come to the restaurant with me before I drop of thirst?" pleaded Ewen, as she ogled a huge tower of chocolates in the food hall.

The restaurant was quite full by the time they had taken the lift upstairs to the fourth floor. A waiter showed them to a table and handed them the menus.

"So much to choose from," sighed Moira, who could not decide between Earl grey tea or *lapsang souchong*. "Now, shall I have a cake or a sandwich?"

Ewen was too busy scanning the restaurant to answer.

Suddenly, he let out a cry,

"Why, look? It's Lord Kinross! I must go and pay my respects. It's a long, long time since we last met."

He jumped up from the table and hurried over to the other side of the restaurant.

Moira could see that the gentleman in question was sitting with two young ladies. He was tall and handsome with wild wavy hair that even though it was cut short, did not sit close to his head. His complexion was ruddy and suggested indulgence rather than health and Moira was not altogether sure that she liked the look of him.

Ewen came bounding over, his face full of enthusiasm.

"Lord Kinross bids us join him for tea. You must come and meet him."

"But Ewen, I thought that the purpose of our outing was to make new plans?"

"Aye, aye, we can talk in the carriage on the way home."

Reluctantly, Moira rose from her seat and followed Ewen to Lord Kinross's table.

"This is my sister, Moira. And Moira, this is Lord Kinross and his two cousins, I am sorry, ladies, but I did not catch your names?"

The two girls simpered. Ewen's charm had won them already, it would seem.

"I am Emily Tennant and this is my cousin, May," said the blonde girl with the fetching curls. She smiled shyly at Moira and inclined her head. Moira thought her charming and she noticed that Ewen was smiling at her a great deal.

"Now, Lady Moira, where have you been hiding your fine brother?" bellowed Lord Kinross. He seemed unable to converse in anything softer than a shout. "I have not seen him for many a long month. Last time, he took my shirt when we played cards. Aye, that was an evening I will not forget."

He laughed loudly and Moira noticed that some ladies who sat nearby turned and tutted. She felt a little embarrassed to be sitting with him.

"The estate has taken up much of my time," said Ewen, "we have had floods and the harvest came in late."

"Ah, the estate. I cannot say that I have seen much of mine lately," replied Lord Kinross, loudly.

The two cousins giggled and once again Moira noticed Emily casting shy glances at Ewen.

"I have lately been in France," continued their host, "and what a time I had in Paris. Ewen, you must visit. The *Folies Bergere*, the *Moulin Rouge* – a man can be treated like a man in Paris and find many amusements to suit his own particular tastes – "

Moira blushed at the innuendo and turned her attention to the trolley of cakes that was being offered by the waiter. Ewen seemed to find his friend hysterically amusing and the two swapped stories while the ladies ate and drank tea in silence.

"Tell me, Ewen," Emily finally spoke, "I have a fancy to see the Highlands. Do you think a lady such as I would find it interesting?"

Ewen turned his gaze upon the young girl. She had sparkling blue eyes and her voice was soft and gentle.

"Why, yes, indeed. The scenery is magnificent and there is riding and hunting, if you are of a mind to do so. If it's shopping you are after, then Edinburgh would prove most worthwhile."

"Lord Kinross is always inviting us to his house in Stirling, but we have yet to find the time. London life is so hectic, do you not find?" Emily asked him.

"Aye, I have been to more parties in the past month than I could count sheep!"

"What brings you down here? It is hard to believe that we have not had the pleasure of seeing you in London before."

"No, it is my first time. We are staying with the Cunninghams for a wee while – "

"I expect you'll be heading back to Lednock for Christmas?" asked Lord Kinross, demolishing a whole choux bun in one mouthful.

"Why, no," piped up Moira, "we are staying indefinitely. We have some business to attend to that has yet to be completed."

She glanced over at Emily as she spoke and noticed that the girl wore a thrilled expression as she looked at Ewen.

'If my brother plays his cards right, he could well have acquired a new admirer,' thought Moira and then vaguely wondered about Lord Kinross. He did not exactly please her, but he was Scottish and rich.

"Well, you must both come to our party tomorrow evening," cried Lord Kinross, slapping his thigh. "It is naught but a few friends and a little music provided by a classical trio, but you will find it most amusing."

"And will you be attending, too?" Ewen asked of the two shy girls.

"Yes, we will," answered Emily, not giving her cousin a chance to reply.

"Good, it is decided!" shouted Lord Kinross. "You are familiar with Cheyne Walk in Chelsea? My house is there – just a modest abode but large enough for a gathering. Ewen, perhaps we can play a hand or two while the ladies chatter?"

Moira dug Ewen in the ribs.

She did not want him gambling what little money they had left. She knew that it would not be possible for them to write home for more.

"Och, I cannot say, George," replied Ewen, sheepishly.

Moira was indeed relieved, but wondered if the smiling Emily had anything to do with his sudden change of heart. She knew that Ewen loved to play cards whenever he had the opportunity.

"But you will come, won't you?" persisted Emily. "I will have no other to accompany me in to dinner, if you would just say yes – "

"Of course," agreed Ewen, blushing, "I would be delighted."

'I must say, these London girls are rather forward,' thought Moira, as she drank her Earl Grey tea, 'in Edinburgh, she would be considered somewhat unladylike.'

"Of course, now that I am engaged, I am not allowed to play cards as much as I used to. Aye, the chains of commitment have finally caught up with me."

Lord Kinross let out another hearty laugh and Moira felt a little put out.

'Well, that is another little fantasy to be exploded,' she said to herself, but deep down, she could not really see herself taking up with such a loud irreverent fellow. She preferred the quieter sort – someone like Stuart.

"Congratulations!" said Ewen, standing up and shaking Lord Kinross's hand feverishly. "Who is the lucky young lady?"

"Celia Trelawney. Her father is a court painter and her mother has a substantial income from the family business. She is the most beautiful girl I have ever seen and she is a feisty lass. I find her amusing company."

Moira noticed that Lord Kinross had mentioned the lady in question's fortune before he had listed her other attributes.

'Money is so important in these circles. No one should think ill of us, then, seeking to improve our situation through marriage.'

She had been brought up to believe in love above all, but here in London, it would seem, it was about making a good match for financial reasons first and foremost.

'Where does love come into his equation?' she wondered, as Lord Kinross continued to extol his intended's more material virtues.

After a while, Moira felt quite tired. The noise and the crowds were too much for a simple Scottish girl like her and she whispered to Ewen that she wished to leave. He seemed most reluctant to go.

"But I have so much to catch up with George."

"Sarah will be back soon and I think it would be nice if we were there to greet her."

"You are going?" put in Emily, unable to hide the disappointment in her voice.

"Yes, I am afraid we must – the friends with whom we are staying are due to return from a funeral."

"Ah, that would be the Bramptons," said Emily. "I had heard of their terrible tragedy. Now, Ewen, you're not going to let me down, are you? We will see you and your charming sister for dinner tomorrow at half-past seven."

Ewen bowed to Emily and the silent May and then shook Lord Kinross's hand.

"We will be there, I promise."

*

Back in the carriage, all that Ewen could talk about was Emily.

"A fine young lassie," he enthused, "and most attractive. I found her gentle manner appealing and her eyes are so blue."

"I gathered that you were impressed with her."

Ewen coloured a little.

127

"Sister, do you think I was too attentive? Will I have put her off?"

"No, dearest, I do believe that she was equally interested. Did you not see how she stared at you all through our tea?"

"Och, I cannot wait to see her tomorrow. I did not know of George's betrothal. The lassie must be a very special woman, George is quite a handful."

"Yes, I did notice. I was quite shocked when he spoke of his adventures in Paris."

"Aye, he always has been one for the ladies, which is why I am surprised that he intends to wed."

"And you, Ewen, do you think that Emily might be a likely candidate for the post of your wife?"

He sighed deeply.

"It all rests on whether she is from a good rich family. If she is related to George, then it is likely, but we will need to investigate her further. Do you think Sarah will ken more of her background?"

"Most likely, she seems to know most people in London Society. We shall ask her this very evening, shall we not?"

Moira hugged her brother's arm and tried not think about Stuart.

They had not been back at Curzon Street for very long, when the sound of carriage wheels was heard in the road outside.

Moira looked out of the window and saw that it was indeed the Cunninghams returning from the funeral.

'Maybe I should put on my lavender wool dress out of respect,' she worried. 'It would seem insensitive to be wearing my plaid at a time like this.'

She took her lavender dress out of the wardrobe and changed quickly.

Running down the stairs, she intercepted Lady Cunningham in the hallway.

"Ah, Moira, dear, how lovely to see you. I have grown quite tired of looking at wan faces. It is a pleasure to see someone so obviously in rude health."

"Yes, I am feeling very well, thank you."

Lady Cunningham gave her one of her searching looks.

"Maybe you have met a special someone?" she asked, dropping her voice so that her husband could not hear.

"No, sadly not. But I think *Ewen* has."

"How thrilling!" declared Lady Cunningham. "Let me go upstairs and change and I will order tea in the drawing room. We shall let the men talk of horses and hounds in the library Laurence will be glad of some male company after my chatter."

Moira could see that Lord Cunningham had indeed taken Ewen into the library. Very soon, the smell of cigarettes was wafting down the corridor.

She waited in the drawing room and presently Lady Cunningham returned.

"It was most thoughtful of you to wear half mourning," she said, gratefully. "Very sensitive of you."

The two women sat down and Berbridge brought in the tea.

"It was such a sad occasion," explained Lady Cunningham. "The family is much depleted now."

"Do you know who will inherit the estates?"

"There was talk of some distant relative but I did not like to pry. I received the impression that until the gentleman in question could be contacted, the family did not wish to discuss it. I only hope that the poor Duchess will not find herself homeless. A worse fate cannot befall a lady."

Moira remained silent.

It reminded her of the desperate state of affairs back at home. In a matter of weeks that could very well be the fate of her own mother and she did not care to dwell upon the matter.

"But, let us talk of more pleasant things. This young lady that Ewen has met, tell me more about her."

"She is a cousin of Lord Kinross and I believe her name is Emily Tennant. Do you know of her family at all?"

Moira tried to phrase her sentence as casually as possible. She did not want her to know how important the information was.

Lady Cunningham sipped her tea and thought for a while before finally speaking,

"Ah, yes, the Tennants. *Nouveau riche*, but a totally charming family. Her father, Edward Tennant, made his fortune in spices from the Far East – China and so on. He owns a large shipping company in the London Docks. I am surprised to hear that Emily is coming out in Society considering she was so ill recently."

Moira's relief at hearing that Emily was a rich heiress was slightly tempered by the last piece of information. Surely she was not a sickly girl?

"Is she ailing?" she asked nervously.

"No, but she suffered from terrible quinsy and was ill for many months. I had heard that she was better, but did not realise that she was fit enough to go out. That is good news, indeed. Her father will be pleased – he is keen for her to make a match before she is much older. I believe she is nearly twenty-one."

Moira could not wait to tell Ewen the news, but had to content herself with more chatter about who had been at the funeral.

As dinnertime approached, she rose to go and see cook.

Moira ran to the library, hoping that Ewen was on his own.

Peeking around the library door, she was pleased to see that Lord Cunningham was asleep in his favourite chair, while Ewen was quietly reading a book.

"Psst! *Ewen.*"

Moira beckoned to her brother to join her in the corridor outside. Ewen crept out of the library and closed the door behind him.

"What is it, sister?"

"Good news. I have been speaking to Sarah about Emily Tennant."

"And?"

"She is indeed a rich heiress and she is without suitors. It would appear that she was ill recently and has been out of circulation for many months. Sarah said that her father is most anxious for her to make a match soon."

"That could not be better news, but I must not tarry with my suit as there could be other young men who have set their caps at her."

Moira hugged her brother. It would seem that the tide had turned in their favour.

"Dearest, I am so pleased for you. Promise me that you will do your best to woo her. But be gentle as she has been ill and will not be ready for too much ardour."

Ewen picked up his sister and wheeled her round, grinning widely.

"Sister, our fortunes have changed for the better. But there is something I wish to discuss with *you*."

Moira suddenly felt concerned. What could it be? Her brother was not a man prone to hasty action, so whatever it was he wanted to say to her, he would have considered it long and hard.

Leading her into the drawing room, he sat her down and joined her on the sofa.

"Dearest sister, I am not an insensitive man and it has been most apparent to me that you have no heart for this marriage game."

"But Ewen, we made an agreement – "

"Hush. I wish to speak, so let me. Moira, I want happiness for you more than anything and there is plenty of time for you to find a husband."

Moira opened her mouth to protest, but Ewen gently placed his fingers on her lips.

"Dearest, should things work out as I believe they will with Emily, we can return home and consider that we have achieved our mission. No arguing with me! I have made my decision."

Moira threw her arms around Ewen's neck and hugged him. He was such a wonderful brother.

"But what if things do not turn out with Emily? There is so much resting on her that I do not care to think of how depressed we shall feel should it all come to naught."

"Moira, I have never felt like this before. I am sure that Emily is the one and that she feels the same way. Trust me, sister. I always knew I would recognise my future wife when I saw her and I do believe that Emily is she."

"Thank you, thank you so much," whispered Moira, full of gratitude.

'Thank you,' she repeated secretly, 'for now I can pursue my dream of Stuart Weston. But how will I find him? And can I be sure that he will return my feelings?'

As Ewen chattered excitedly about their plans for the following evening, Moira was suddenly beset with fear.

Ewen had given her a way out of having to make a match for the sake of money, but now that she was free to follow her dream, she felt so many doubts.

'What if Stuart rejects me? I have scant evidence that he feels for me any emotion other than friendship. I could not bear to make myself vulnerable to him, only to have him cast me aside'

It was with these anxieties coursing through her mind that Moira retired to bed.

'Could I really win my heart's desire?' she pondered, as she brushed out her hair ready to slide in between the sheets. 'Is it just possible that Stuart may harbour the same feelings for me as I do for him?'

Moira could not wait for Ewen to come to a successful conclusion to his quest and then they could return home on Stuart's ship.

'I do not think I can wait that long,' she thought, snuggling up in the feather pillows, 'and what will we find when we return to Lednock?'

As a result of her mind churning, Moira spent a sleepless night.

Part of their mission was on its way to being accomplished, but the worst could still lie ahead.

CHAPTER NINE

The next day Moira brooded a great deal about her situation. She found herself feeling almost guilty that Ewen had given her a way out of having to make a financial marriage as well.

Finally she came to a decision.

Ewen was in the library poring over some of Lord Cunningham's collection of maps. Moira knocked and hearing Ewen's voice, put her head around the door.

"Ah, Moira. Do come and see these maps. They're grand. Sixteenth century. This one even has Loch Earn village marked on it."

"There is something I wish to discuss with you."

"Aye, what is it?"

"Ewen, I have been giving a great deal of consideration to the matter we discussed last night."

He looked at her blankly.

"Heavens," she said, impatiently. "You suggested that there was no need for me to make a match purely for money. Well, I have thought about it and I do not think it fair that you should carry the burden. We shall proceed as planned."

Ewen rose and hugged his sister.

"No, you will do no such thing! I have made my mind up and that is the way it shall stay. If Emily is willing to allow me to woo her and matters run their course, you shall have no need of an enforced marriage. That is my final word on it, sister."

Moira knew that once Ewen had decided upon something, nothing could sway him.

She left the library, secretly filled with joy. Even the thought of the impending party at Lord Kinross's house no longer burdened her.

Ewen, she noticed, was eagerly looking forward to it. That morning at breakfast, he had barely touched his food – a sure sign that he was excited about the evening to come.

In spite of feeling more relaxed, Moira was still a little apprehensive at her lack of suitable clothes. But now that she was no longer on the hunt for a husband, wearing the apricot chiffon one more time really did not seem such a problem.

*

The day passed quickly.

Moira spent most of her time with Lady Cunningham who was making preparations for Christmas. It was barely a week away now and she and Ewen had an open invitation to stay for the celebrations should they desire.

There had been another letter from her mother, but she had had very little to say, apart from the fact that there had been no change in her father and that they were coping well under the circumstances.

Moira wished that she could return home, even if it meant leaving Ewen behind to woo Emily. She did not think she would miss Mayfair and she knew that her mother would be overjoyed to see her again.

"Are you looking forward to the party this evening?" asked Lady Cunningham, interrupting Moira's train of thought.

"Why, yes, I do believe I am," she replied, thinking of how Ewen had told her that Lord Kinross's parties were always splendidly informal affairs.

"Perhaps tonight will bring you luck."

"I think that Ewen is the one who is really excited about this evening."

"Ah, Emily Tennant? I do hope that all goes well this evening. I cannot see how she could fail to fall for such a handsome young man. But there will be many disappointed others should he be taken."

Moira smiled. It was true, Ewen had collected quite a few hearts during their short stay, but he seemed blissfully unaware of them.

"Dear, I will not keep you any longer as it is almost after five. I suggest that you go upstairs and start getting ready."

Moira hurried back to her room where the maid had already laid out her apricot chiffon after sponging it down. It looked almost new again thanks to her tender care. Taking down her vanity case from the top of the wardrobe, Moira found the pale blue box containing her mother's diamonds.

'The last of a very fine collection and if Ewen's plan goes to order, mother can replace some of the other pieces she has been forced to sell. God willing.'

*

The carriage taking them to Lord Kinross's residence arrived at seven o'clock sharp. Ewen told Moira that his friend lived in a rather unfashionable area, called Chelsea.

"It is full of ordinary people and many artists, sculptors, actors and singers," he explained, as their carriage set off. "It is not as smart as Mayfair, but I'll warrant that he has some interesting types for neighbours. Aye, George has always preferred the company of colourful people."

"I hear that he likes to frequent the theatre. Perhaps we shall be graced with the likes of Sarah Bernhardt or Dan Leno the clog dancer."

"Moira! He is not to be found in the supper rooms or East End taverns. George has more breeding than that. You have a vivid imagination."

Moira had a notion that Lord Kinross was in the habit of befriending what Sarah would describe as '*bohemians*', but she tried to keep her mind as open as possible.

It was a chilly night and a mist was beginning to rise from the Thames as their carriage pulled up outside Lord Kinross's house.

Moira was surprised that it did not appear at all grand from its exterior and that fact, in a strange way, made her feel less anxious.

'No one will be casting critical eyes over my gown tonight,' she thought.

As they walked up the path towards the open front door, Ewen hissed in her ear,

"Of course, you know that George keeps a mistress. An artist's model who lives nearby. I hope that he has not invited both her and his fiancée tonight otherwise there will be hell to pay!"

Moira felt shocked. How could Lord Kinross even entertain such an idea? Surely it went against all taste and decency?

She had heard rumours when in Edinburgh that there were gentlemen who had 'kept women' as well as wives, but in her innocence had dismissed it as idle gossip.

As soon as she entered the door of the house in Cheyne Walk, she could tell that the people who flitted around inside like exotic butterflies were a world away from the stiff snooty crowd whom she had met over the past few weeks.

There was an altogether more relaxed atmosphere at Lord Kinross's home and looking around, she noticed that not every woman present was wearing the latest bustle.

"Why, the old rascal," whispered Ewen, as they entered the large drawing room. "Look, that yon lassie with the dark hair and fine figure – that is George's mistress!"

She looked over to the other side of the room and there, dressed in a strange yet becoming gown was a haughty looking woman of about twenty-six standing by an impressive Davenport.

She wore a mass of feathers in her hair that hung loose down her back, and sported a large Chinese jade pendant on her bosom that drew attention to the fact that she was not wearing a corset.

Moira noticed that the woman followed George with the eyes of a hawk, yet she did not attempt to accost him. She had never seen a mistress before and she could not help but stare.

It was only the arrival of Emily and May Tennant that took her attention away from the fascinating creature by the Davenport.

Ewen caught his breath as Emily arrived in the drawing room – she looked quite beautiful with her blonde curls piled high on her head and a sprinkling of diamonds that were just enough to make her sparkle in a subtle way.

Her dress was pale lemon chiffon and quite put Moira's old gown into the shade.

"Moira, will you pardon me while I go and greet Miss Tennant?" said Ewen, breathless with excitement.

"Of course, dearest. However, please do not leave me on my own all night as I fear I do not know anyone here."

Ewen gave her a grin and then darted over to where Emily and May were standing.

Moira watched as Emily smiled shyly and put her head on one side while Ewen talked to her.

"Ah, you must be the Scots girl," came a piercing voice behind her.

There was a tug on Moira's elbow and she turned to find a trio of elderly ladies.

"I am, Agnes, Sarah Cunningham's sister-in-law and she has told me about you."

Moira graciously nodded at the three ladies and smiled politely, hoping that they would disappear. But to her dismay Agnes grabbed her by the arm and dragged her out into the connecting dining room.

It was informally set for a musical recital with a long buffet table groaning with food along one side.

At the end of the room stood a grand piano and two chairs and leaning against one was a cello while a violin was laid across the other.

Lord Kinross obviously took no notice of the polite social code that dictated that pianos should be covered with a chenille cloth and decorated with at least a candelabrum and a vase of flowers, for his was completely bare of any such embellishments.

"Yes, shocking, isn't it?" commented Agnes, pointing at the offending instrument as if it were a naked statue rather than a piano.

"He only invites us because he knows we will be scandalised," cried her friend.

"Well, I find him refreshing and unstuffy," put in the third. "What say you, young lady?"

"I could not say. We do not have a piano at Lednock – my father prefers us to play the harp."

"The harp," enthused Agnes. "How delightful."

"Such quaint ways, the Scots," added her friend, "do tell us more about your charming country."

And so, Moira spent the first part of the evening fielding questions about her culture from haggis to bagpipes to kilts.

"And I do hear that the new Duke of Brampton is a distant cousin who hails from your country," said Agnes suddenly. "It was such a terrible shock to all of us, hearing of both untimely ends. And then comes news of this heir who is not known to any of us. I do hope he is not some ruffian from the bogs!"

Moira suddenly snapped out of her torpor and seized upon what she was saying.

"Do you mean that the new Duke is a Scot?"

"Yes, my dear. Perhaps you will know him? Now, if only I could remember his name. I declare it does not sound Scottish at all which is why I cannot recall it."

Agnes was infuriatingly vague and waved her hand in the air as if to conjure up the name from the ether.

"Scotland is not so vast," answered Moira. "I may well be acquainted with his kin at the very least. There are relatively few good families in my area and we all know each other it is not like London."

"No! No. The name has gone," fluttered Agnes, "perhaps I will remember after the musical recital. I do so

141

find that music soothes me and all kinds of memories come flooding back."

"But, Agnes, dear, have you not heard? It is rumoured that George Kinross has invited the new Duke to this very event," intervened her friend, "so perhaps the young lady will have the pleasure of renewing an old acquaintance."

Moira suddenly felt rather excited.

'Who could this elusive stranger be?' she wondered.

She knew practically everyone there was to know in the social scene in Edinburgh and Glasgow and it was not beyond the realms of possibility that she had indeed already met him in the past.

'Perhaps he could prove to be a prospective suitor,' mused Moira, as the gong sounded to summon them into the dining room.

Moira became so excited that she ate only a small amount from the large buffet.

Ewen came over to her, his face aglow with happiness.

"Moira. There you are. Where have you been?"

"Talking to Lady Cunningham's sister-in-law and I found out a rather interesting piece of news the new Duke of Brampton is Scottish. It is rumoured that he has been invited to this very party. Now, what do you think of *that*?"

"Och, I cannot take much interest in women's gossip," he chided, "as I am making such good progress with Emily. She has accepted my invitation to go out walking tomorrow and she has invited me to her father's shoot after Christmas."

Moira squeezed her brother's arm warmly.

"Dearest, that is wonderful news. So we will be staying on after all?"

"Aye, we will. I shall send a telegram to mother and father tomorrow and let them know of our decision."

"They will be disappointed."

"But not when I take Emily back as my fiancée," he cried, his eyes full of joy. "And then we can snatch back Lednock from the hands of those evil creditors!"

The butler announced the musical recital and Ewen and Moira took their seats next to Lord Kinross and his fiancée. Emily and May shyly followed and sat next to Ewen.

Moira was amused to note that Lord Kinross's mistress was sitting behind them, glaring daggers at his intended. She wondered if there would be a scene at some point during the evening –

"Are you enjoying yourself, my dear?" Lord Kinross asked of Moira.

"Yes, I am indeed. But what is this news I hear that the new Duke of Brampton is to be present tonight?

"Why yes, he was meant to be here, but so far he has not graced us with is presence. I expect that he has been detained on some urgent business. He is a lucky man – the Brampton fortune and estates are considerable."

Just then, the pianist arrived in the room to polite applause and curtailed Moira's chance to make further enquiries.

She felt quite disappointed that the new Duke had so far not shown his face as she had been sufficiently piqued by Agnes's chatter to nurture hopes that if he was unmarried, she might wheedle an introduction.

After playing for around twenty minutes, the musicians took a bow before announcing that they would resume playing again after a short interval.

Moira had just resumed chatting to Lord Kinross when his butler interrupted them.

"Begging your pardon, my Lord, but His Grace the Duke of Brampton has just arrived. He is in the hall. I wondered whether you wished me to bring him through."

"No, I will come and greet him myself," was the hearty reply, "and bring my best Napoleon brandy as I must drink to his health."

"A late arrival?" asked Moira, as calmly as she could.

"Yes, better late than never."

Lord Kinross arose from his chair, his eyebrows raised expectantly. Moira could hardly bear to look, so she averted her gaze away from the entrance to the dining room.

Ewen was deep in conversation with Emily as Moira casually scanned the room.

It was not long before she spotted a newcomer.

'Surely it cannot be. No. This is a miracle,' she thought, as her eyes alighted on a familiar figure with reddish-brown, flowing hair and penetrating pale blue eyes.

There, standing by the door and conversing jovially with Lord Kinross was none other than *Stuart Weston*!

Stuart caught Moira's eye and his face lit up.

Her heart was beating hard in her chest and her mouth became dry as Stuart walked over to where she was sitting.

"You!" she stuttered, at last. "What are you doing here and where is the new Duke of Brampton? Do you know him? Is he a friend of yours?"

"*You are looking at him*," answered Stuart, bowing low, his blue eyes dancing.

"Ah, I see that you two know each other already. You have deprived me of an introduction," blustered Lord Kinross, as the butler brought in a bottle of brandy.

Stuart took the seat next to Moira and looked at her longingly.

"I cannot believe it is you! How? *Why*?" she whispered.

"Hush, I will you tell you more later," he replied softly as the music resumed.

But Moira could not concentrate on what the trio was playing, no matter how fine it was as her thoughts were utterly consumed by Stuart.

'Stuart. *Oh, my love*. How I have longed for this moment.'

She could not help but steal peeks at him and she noticed that he was always looking at her, his eyes telling her that he had missed her.

'I cannot wait for this recital to be over,' thought Moira impatiently. The trio was now playing a pretty little Chopin *etude*, but she could not enjoy it, even though it was one of her favourites.

It was some time before Ewen realised that his dear friend had joined the party.

In fact, the recital had drawn to a close and Moira was just about to quiz Stuart on how fate had brought him to Chelsea, when Ewen noticed him.

"Kelpie!" he roared, "what brings you here?"

"It is a long story, old friend."

'Oh, I do hope that Ewen will not keep him long,' thought Moira, annoyed at having Stuart's attention snatched away from her by her brother. 'I have not seen Stuart in over a month and there is so much I need to discuss with him.'

But still they talked and joked.

The next moment Ewen was introducing Emily and May to Stuart, much to Moira's dismay.

"You are in town for a few days, I hope?" asked Ewen, his attention beginning to return to Emily. "I hope you are still sailing the *Victorious* or we will be stranded here."

"Yes, I am and she remains at your disposal. But judging by the look of that charming young lady on your arm, you will be in no hurry to leave London."

Ewen laughed heartily and patted Emily's hand.

"And I must no longer ignore this charming young lady, if you will excuse me, Kelpie. I will speak more with you later."

Moira could have cried with relief as Ewen led Emily away with May in hot pursuit. She had been so afraid that Stuart would be distracted by them.

Now she had him to herself at last.

"Moira," began Stuart, leading her away from the dining room, "I would speak with you in private."

"Of course, but are you not expected to circulate as the new Duke of Brampton?"

"That can wait and what I have to say to you will not. Shall we find a quiet corner in this madhouse away from the rest of the guests?"

"Would that – not be rude?" stammered Moira.

'Why I am behaving like such a fool?' she thought, 'I have waited forever for Stuart to return and now I find myself making excuses not to be alone with him. What is wrong with me?'

But Stuart was not easily put off.

He took Moira's arm and made her follow him into Lord Kinross's study.

Bidding her to sit on the sofa, Stuart sank down next her, taking her hand in his. Moira's heart was bursting with emotion.

"Moira, dearest Moira – I cannot tell you how overjoyed I am to see you and how sorry I am that I did not honour my promise to write to you."

"It is of no consequence."

"Hush. Let me say my piece."

Admonished, Moira fell silent whilst Stuart continued,

"I said that I was terrible at remembering names and addresses and I fear that is exactly what I did. No sooner had you left the *Victorious* than the name of the people who you were staying with went right out of my head. Try as I might, I could not recall it and I could not be so bold as to trouble your parents, so I resigned myself to losing you forever to someone else!"

Realising what Stuart was saying, Moira looked into his eyes, her own so full of love that she felt utterly vulnerable and open to him.

"Oh, Stuart," she murmured.

"It came as a complete shock to me. One day, I was sailing my ship up and down the coast and the next, I was a Duke! I knew that the Bramptons were distant kin of mine on my father's side, but had never given it so much as a thought. My second cousin was the heir and the question of what would happen should he die had not arisen.

"Then the awful accident occurred and word was sent North. I was in Perth when the messenger came and I did not think it was true until I was summoned to the lawyer in

London. Overnight, my fortunes had changed and my first thought was to find you!"

"Stuart, I had not realised that you had feelings for me. All these long weeks without a letter made me draw the conclusion that you cared not one jot for me."

"How wrong you are, dearest Moira," cried Stuart, tightening his grip on her hand. "How very, very wrong!"

"But you had given me no signal and nothing to hope for. So you will forgive my bewilderment."

Stuart sighed and hung his head.

"I am not a forward man when it comes to matters of love. I have had little experience, having preferred the life of a sea captain, coming and going as I pleased. That first day in the garden when I saw you – it was then that I realised that perhaps what I was searching for was not to be found on the ocean."

"You knew so early?" questioned Moira, in wonderment. "I must confess that from the beginning, you did rather turn my head. I found you so dashing and gentlemanly."

As they gazed into each other's eyes, they were rudely interrupted by a group of boisterous guests crashing into the study.

"Sorry, old boy. We were looking for George's cigar humidor. I know he keeps it in here somewhere."

"Come," whispered Stuart, "let us go out into the garden, if you think you can bear the cold."

"I am a true Highland lass," said Moira, "the cold is second nature to me."

They walked into the small courtyard garden through the back door.

The stars were shining brilliantly in the clear evening sky and the moon was high and huge.

Stuart took Moira's hands and rubbed them to keep them from the cold.

"Darling Moira, I have missed you beyond words. You cannot understand how much it means to me to be here with you now. I feared that by the time I arrived, some young man would have claimed you for his own."

"No, never! I have thought of no other but you since the day we first met. But circumstances conspired against us."

Stuart looked at her with a puzzled expression.

"Darling, I am afraid I fail to understand what you mean."

Moira cast her eyes away. She could not tell Stuart of her family's misfortunes.

"It is nothing, a mere trifle," she murmured, squeezing his hand so tightly.

"When I arrived here this evening and saw you again, I realised that we were meant to be together," Stuart declared. "I almost did not dare to hope that you would still be unbetrothed."

"My dearest, there has never been any other – "

Stuart sighed and pulled her closer. She sank into his arms, her heart bursting with happiness.

"Darling, before this unfortunate series of events that led to me inheriting the Brampton fortune, I did not dare ask you. I am now a man of substantial means and I am certain that your father would not object to my suit, so *please will you marry me?*"

Moira was overjoyed.

149

"Oh, but I have longed for nothing less," she cried. "My answer is *yes*, Stuart, I will be your wife."

"Darling," he murmured, closing his eyes, his lips drawing close to hers.

Holding her close in the moonlight, he kissed her.

Moira had never known such ecstasy.

She melted into his embrace and felt the world spinning.

Quite dizzy, she composed herself. Stuart was smiling down at her, his firm, strong arms holding her tightly.

"Darling, I know that you are young, but there is no time to waste. I cannot be a Duke without a wife. Let us return to Scotland immediately and I shall seek your father's permission for us to marry at once. We can leave tomorrow – the *Victorious* lies waiting at Tilbury, if only you would say yes."

Moira thought for a second.

She had promised Ewen that they would stay for Christmas so that he might woo Emily. But if *she* now had a chance to save Lednock, surely he could not object to her leaving early?

'With Stuart at my side, we shall overcome all our difficulties,' she sighed to herself, as once more he pulled her close and kissed her.

With the moon still shining brightly overhead and the stars twinkling, Moira felt that this is just what Heaven must be like.

Lost in the richness of love, she could not wait to tell Ewen that their troubles were now over –

CHAPTER TEN

The rest of the evening was a heady blur for Moira.

She felt as if she was walking on air as she and Stuart returned to the drawing room. Ewen was utterly absorbed with Emily and Moira could see that things were going very well indeed.

Emily smiled shyly at her as she walked towards them. Her eyes were shining and Moira could tell by the looks that she cast at Ewen that she was already very much in love with him.

'I could not wish for a better evening,' she thought happily, as her brother turned round to greet her.

"Sister. There you are. Emily is about to leave and wants to say goodbye."

"Yes, indeed. I do so hope that we can become friends, Moira," said Emily quietly.

"I would like to very much," replied Moira.

"Ah, Stuart," trumpeted Ewen, noticing him standing nearby, "I haven't had the opportunity to talk with you, but perhaps we can meet tomorrow?"

"I am afraid that will not be possible, Ewen, for I am forced to return home to Perth tomorrow. There are some urgent matters that require my attention. Now, if you will excuse me? Lady Moira – "

He kissed Moira's hand and gave her a meaningful look. He had promised her that he would call on her at Curzon Street the next day to make plans for their journey North.

Ewen tarried over his goodbyes to Emily, whilst Moira sat in the carriage, impatient to tell him her news while he dilly-dallied by Emily's carriage, kissing her hand a hundred times and promising to call on her.

Eventually, he tore himself away and sat down next to Moira.

"I did not think I could fall in love so hard," he exclaimed, as he stretched out on the seat. "I feel as if I have wings! Do you not think that Emily is the most beautiful and delightful girl in the whole of London?"

"Of course she is, brother, she is your love," said Moira smiling, "now if you will hush for a while, I have something important to tell *you*."

"You have? Has my wee sister met someone? Och, that will teach me for taking no notice of you all night."

"Ewen, please listen. Yes, it is true, I have met someone and what is more, you know him."

"I do?" Ewen was leaning forward, his face full of curiosity.

"Yes, it is Stuart Weston. The new Duke of Brampton. Furthermore, he has asked me to marry him. Ewen, our troubles are all over. We leave for Scotland tomorrow on the *Victorious* so that he may ask father for my hand."

Ewen looked startled rather than delighted by her wonderful news.

"But Moira, you cannot go without a chaperone, it would not be right. Think of the scandal."

"I do not care for scandal and gossip and since when have you stood on ceremony? Stuart is the perfect gentleman and there will no impropriety. In any case, who is going to be onboard to spy on us and tittle-tattle?"

Ewen fell silent.

Moira could see that something was troubling him. Was there something about Stuart that he needed to tell her and was trying to find a way to break the news gently?

Moira could stand it no longer.

"Ewen, for Heaven's sake, if Stuart has some dark secret in his past, will you please tell me at once. I cannot bear this."

"Oh, sister, pardon my reticence," he began, "but if you are intending to leave tomorrow for Scotland, then I am sorry but I cannot go with you. I wish to stay longer and woo Emily. Would you mind if you went alone? I am sure one of the servants could chaperone you if necessary."

"Is that all that is ailing you? Of course I will not mind if you stay and firm your suit with Emily. I am sure that Sarah will be delighted that at least one of us is staying and I expect that Emily will be invited over for tea with her?

"I do not think that we should make your engagement public, Moira not even to Sarah. At least, not until father has given his consent. Aye, I worry for what you might find when you return home."

It was now Moira's turn to fall silent. In all her excitement, she had not considered whether or not her father would even be fit enough to receive Stuart.

'What if father does not want to see him?' she pondered. 'We do not have any time to lose and any delay could result in us being evicted from Lednock.'

She did not mention her fears to Ewen. A solution to their problems was so near, yet so far. Instead, she retired as soon as they returned to Curzon Street.

Moira was tired, yet she could not sleep. Her mind was whirling as she tried to imagine what would happen when she brought Stuart back, but this time as her intended.

'Mother will be delighted and she will remember him from the hunting party we held when Larry Harwood was staying. But when shall I break the news to Stuart of my family's awful predicament?'

It was this thought more than any other that kept her awake for many hours. It seemed that no sooner had she fallen asleep than the maid was knocking on her door.

'I must look my best for Stuart,' she said to herself, dressing hastily. Her reflection in the dressing table mirror did not please her. She looked almost as wan as May Tennant!

Pinching her cheeks furiously, Moira put on her plaid dress and went downstairs.

Lady Cunningham smiled as she walked into the dining room.

"Good morning, my dear. I trust you had a good evening?"

"Yes, I enjoyed myself immensely. Although I declare that the company Lord Kinross keeps is colourful to say the least. However, I did have the pleasure of meeting your sister-in-law, Agnes."

"Ah, Agnes. I do hope that she did not talk you to death. Agnes is rather voluble and she even talked all the way through my and Laurence's wedding!"

They both laughed and Moira took her seat at the table.

"Sarah, a friend of the family will be calling this morning. I do hope it will not inconvenience you in any way. It is urgent business."

"I shall make myself scarce. Is it a handsome young man by any chance?"

"A friend of my brother."

Lady Cunningham was discreet enough not to push Moira for more details, but she could tell by her expression that there was more to this 'visitor' than met the eye.

"And your brother – how did he fare with Miss Tennant?"

"Very well, but there is something I need to tell you. Sarah, I have had such a wonderful time in London but I will not now be staying for Christmas. Something has come up that requires my attention and while Ewen will remain behind, I must travel North this very evening."

"My dear, I am sorry to hear this news. You have become a true friend and I will miss your company. However, I understand the pull of family ties and will have Berbridge make the carriage ready for you."

"Thank you, but there will be no necessity, Sarah," said Moira, reddening with embarrassment, "I have already made my own arrangements."

There was an awkward silence as Lady Cunningham stirred her tea.

Moira felt guilty – she had confided so much in her, yet until her engagement to Stuart had been formally announced, she could not tell her more.

The timely entrance of Berbridge, who formally announced that the Duke of Brampton had arrived to see Lady Moira, broke the awkwardness of the situation.

Moira excused herself and almost ran from the dining room.

"*Darling*," she cried, running into Stuart's arms.

They kissed tenderly and then pulled apart.

"I could barely sleep a wink last night, I was so excited."

Stuart kissed her forehead, and clasped her hands.

"It was the same for me, my angel. So I packed my bags instead and brought them with me. I thought that we could leave as soon as you are ready."

Moira was breathless with elation. If this was a foretaste of what was to come as Stuart's wife, she would surely never become bored.

"Oh, darling. This is such a surprise. But we cannot leave before I have seen Ewen – and I must also make sure that I thank Lady Cunningham for her hospitality."

"Then let us go for a walk and discuss our plans together," suggested Stuart, as practical as ever. "Have the maid pack your trunks and together we will see Lady Cunningham after our walk to explain everything to her. There is a very good flower stall in Bond Street where we can pick up a bouquet for her."

Moira flew upstairs to put on her cloak and boots.

Downstairs, Stuart was waiting for her in the hall. Stepping outside, she felt so proud by his side. She felt sure that passers-by would think him as handsome as she did.

"You realise that we will have to delay the wedding until after Christmas," said Stuart slowly. "I had quite forgotten that a decent period of mourning needs to be observed before our ceremony can take place."

Moira almost stopped short in her tracks. This would not do at all. The family affairs would not wait so long as the creditors were practically at the door already.

'Oh, this cannot be,' she thought. 'How can I save Lednock if there is such a delay? There is nothing for it – I shall have to tell Stuart about our predicament.'

"Darling, is there something troubling you?" enquired Stuart, as they crossed Berkeley Square, "you have not said a word for five minutes. You are upset that the wedding has to be delayed, naturally – "

"Stuart, there is something that you need know. I did not want to tell you but this latest piece of news has forced my hand. My situation is not as rosy as you would perceive it to be. What you witnessed at Lednock earlier in the year was but a sham, put on for Larry Harwood's benefit.

"The truth of the matter is that father travelled to America with him and lost everything. The castle, the estate, our money, our inheritance."

"I knew that Lednock was not as wealthy as it once was, but I had no idea that things were so bad. How could this be?"

Moira sat down on a bench and began to cry.

She dabbed at her eyes, trying to regain her composure. How it distressed her to have to admit to their downfall.

"Harwood promised father that he could treble his money if he invested in some mines near New York. He did not realise that Harwood was a crook who would cheat him out of his lands and home."

Stuart took a deep breath and looked at her in disbelief.

"But this is extortion! Have you informed the police? I am sure that the Earl would not have been the only person to have been fooled by him."

"No, no, that would only make things worse and the scandal would kill father. He is already ill and has taken to his bed. Mother is beside herself with worry. Ewen and I thought that if we came to London and found ourselves rich spouses, perhaps we could buy off Larry Harwood's creditors."

Moira looked nervously at Stuart.

She felt so vulnerable now that she had told him everything.

'I do hope that he will not think that I have feigned love for him in order to get at his new fortune,' she thought, then hurriedly dismissed it. She was confident that hers and Stuart's love was strong enough to overcome any hurdle.

"You must not tell a soul, Stuart, please."

"But Moira. We should alert the authorities."

"Stuart, we cannot. The creditors for the American Bank are due to start dismantling the estate any time now. It is too late – "

Stuart shook his head in dismay.

"If only you had told me sooner, Moira. I could have helped out, even though I do not have the Brampton fortune yet, it is only days away from being mine. I would happily bail out your father.

"Moira looked up at him gratefully. How she loved him!

"Darling, we must concentrate on returning to Lednock as soon as possible. The news of our engagement may well provide a boost to father's well-being. We cannot leave soon enough."

"Then we shall leave this very afternoon. Now, we shall visit the florist and then make haste back to Curzon Street. We can be on our way to Tilbury by lunchtime."

There were a few tears when Moira told Lady Cunningham that her departure had been hastened by Stuart's arrival.

Ewen hugged Moira as the footman loaded up the carriage.

"Darling sister," he murmured, "I will write to you as soon as I have any news. I intend to propose to Emily during the shoot after Christmas, if not sooner. I have a mind to ask her this afternoon!"

Lady Cunningham was delighted with her flowers, but declared that they were no substitute for Moira's fine company.

Ewen came up to the carriage and kissed his sister affectionately "Be sure to look after her, Stuart," he urged. "Sister, I will see you presently."

The driver cracked his whip over the team of horses and the carriage wheeled away from the Cunninghams' residence.

Moira began to weep quietly, much to her surprise. She had become firm friends with Lady Cunningham and had been touched at how upset she was to see her depart.

In spite of her trepidation, Moira was looking forward to returning to Lednock.

'I do hope that the worst has not befallen mother and father,' she thought as the motion of the carriage lulled her senses. 'I do hope we that we arrive in time.'

*

The *Victorious* was moored at Tilbury Docks awaiting their arrival. Moira shivered as she stepped down from the carriage and stood on the quayside.

The crew were running hither and thither, loading huge parcels into the hold.

"We are carrying a cargo of rice, salt and spices," explained Stuart. "Much of it is destined for local shops. It is their winter stock and just in time for Christmas."

It was then that Moira realised that Christmas was but a few days away. They were due to arrive home at Lednock on Christmas Eve and she hoped that her return would be a good present for her parents.

"You will be staying in the same cabin as on the voyage out and I hope that will be acceptable," Stuart said as he helped her up the gangway. "The wind is getting up and I fear that the journey may be rough, so I want you to be as comfortable as possible."

It was true, the wind was whipping Moira's cloak around her and she had difficulty in keeping her hat from blowing away.

"I am sure I will be fine," she muttered, trying to convince herself.

As she descended into the bowels of the ship, she was pleased to find herself untroubled by memories of the awful MacKinnon. He now seemed so utterly unimportant.

Entering the cabin, she thought how different things now were. True, the problem of saving Lednock was still in front of them, but this time there was Stuart at her side.

'I feel as if I could do anything as long as he is with me.'

*

The journey North was terribly difficult.

As Stuart had predicted, the weather worsened and a storm soon blew up.

160

Moira found that she could not control her seasickness and was forced to remain in her cabin, being tended to by Stuart when he could spare time away from the bridge.

As a result, when they finally docked in Dundee, she felt too ill to take the carriage on to Lednock.

Stuart suggested a decent lodging house, completely unlike Mrs. McRae's establishment and he journeyed on to Perth to open up his house, while the amiable Mrs. MacKenzie tended Moira.

The next day dawned bright and cold and Moira awoke feeling so much better. Although her legs were a trifle wobbly, she easily climbed into Stuart's carriage when it arrived to pick her up after breakfast.

"Sir will be waiting for you at his house in Perth," the driver informed her.

Moira was curious to see it but did not have the chance, for as soon as the carriage arrived at the modest house, Stuart ran out to greet her and leapt inside.

"Darling," he exclaimed, kissing her fervently, "how are you this morning? You look so pale and thin."

"I am much better, thank you, and am looking forward to arriving home. How long do you think the journey will take?"

Stuart consulted with the driver. The roads were still hard with frost and the horses could not go at full gallop for fear of their hooves slipping.

"Probably five hours," he reported after much debate. "We shall be lucky to arrive before nightfall."

They set off without Moira having so much as glimpsed the inside of his house.

"I shall be putting the place up for sale as soon as matters are resolved with the Brampton estate," commented Stuart, as they made progress along the cold, country roads. "I have a notion to retain a house in Scotland, but the one in Perth will not be suitable. Especially if we are blessed with children."

Moira blushed to the roots of her hair.

Of course, she wanted a family, but had not given it any thought since it felt like such a distant possibility. Even the thought of her wedding was overshadowed by the prospect of what might lie in wait for her at Lednock.

Stuart sensed her nervousness and did all he could to soothe her.

"Darling, whatever happens, your father and mother will not be thrown out of the castle. I now have the means at my disposal to at least hold off the creditors."

Moira looked up at him with eyes full of gratitude.

"But dearest, I could not ask it of you."

"Moira, your brother is one of my close friends and I have great respect for your father. Do you think I would see my bride's parents thrown into the workhouse? I would not be a man if I did not do something."

As the sun began to sink in the cold grey sky, the scenery became very familiar.

"We are approaching Loch Earn," Moira whispered, almost to herself. "It seems so strange to be coming home London feels like a whole lifetime away."

She watched as darkening fields sped past and soon the turrets of Lednock could be glimpsed at the end of the loch.

'I cannot believe I am almost home,' she thought, her heart hammering hard.

As the carriage rounded the corner just before the entrance to the estate, Moira was puzzled to see what looked like a Police Constable standing by the gate.

Sure enough, as they approached, the carriage suddenly lurched to a halt.

"Who goes there?" hailed the Officer.

The carriage driver turned to Stuart and asked him what he should do. Stuart did not hesitate. He put his head out of the window and shouted to the Officer,

"This carriage bears Lady Moira Strathcarron. Now, let us pass at once."

"Stuart," whispered Moira, becoming increasingly alarmed, "what is going on? Why is there a uniformed Officer at the gate? It is father. I *know* it is."

The Officer walked up to the carriage and held up his lantern.

"Begging your pardon, my Lady," he exclaimed, upon seeing Moira.

He waved the carriage on and Moira clung to Stuart fearfully.

"What *on earth* can be going on?"

"Hush, do not fret," said Stuart soothingly, "we do not know the reason for this and it may not be what you fear. Perhaps there has been a burglary – "

"– or a murder," moaned Moira, now in tears.

As the carriage drew up to the front of the castle, Moira was almost too frightened to alight. Even the comforting sight of Rankin making his way towards her did nothing to dispel her unease.

"My Lady," he said, breaking into a rare smile, "it warms my heart to see you."

"Rankin, can you tell me what is going on? There is an Officer at the gate who did not want to let us through."

"Moira. Darling. What a wonderful surprise!"

Before Rankin had a chance to say anything, the Countess had swept out of the door and ran towards her daughter who was halfway down the carriage steps.

"Mother."

Tears flowed freely as mother and daughter embraced.

Stuart, respectfully, hung back and supervised the unloading of Moira's trunks.

"Mother, you must tell me now. Why is there an Officer at the gate?"

"But you received my telegram, of course?" she replied, looking mystified.

She did not notice Stuart standing nearby, assuming that he was the carriage driver. In the dark, Stuart's distinctive appearance was not apparent.

"No, I have been at sea for four days. What did it say?"

"Come inside, my dear, we should not be discussing matters in front of strangers."

Moira opened her mouth to say that Stuart was no stranger, but he shook his head and put his finger to his lips.

She understood that he recognised that she should delay relating their news, so she allowed her mother to lead her away inside whilst he remained outside.

"Moira, a wonderful, wonderful thing has happened," began her mother, breathlessly. "Yesterday our peace and quiet was shattered by the arrival of an entire carriage-full of Officers and two officials from the American Bank."

"Mother – surely they have not come – to take Lednock?"

"No, darling. Far from it. Larry Harwood has been arrested in Chicago on extortion charges after the American authorities had investigated his affairs. The evil man had fled to Chicago hoping to make a new start.

"When the authorities gained access to his strongbox at the bank, they found the documents and deeds to Lednock. As they are pressing charges, they came directly to Scotland to take a statement from your father.

"Darling, Lednock is saved and Larry Harwood will be languishing in prison for a very long time!"

Moira could not believe what she was hearing.

"Does this mean that we shall not have to leave Lednock and that father has the deeds to the estate once more?"

The Countess smiled.

"Your father is not a stupid man. The original deeds were with his lawyer in Stirling the entire time. Although he took a risk, he was not foolhardy enough to part with the real documents. Harwood would have had a difficult time should he have gone as far as trying to seize the estate as the papers he held were only copies."

"So there was no need for father to have worried so much?"

"Dearest, your father was sick with remorse for what he had done to his family. His mental state was such that he was not thinking coherently – he did not know that copies would not be valid in the eyes of the law should Harwood try to claim the estate."

"Then this is indeed a happy day. Where is father? I must see him immediately."

"I am here, daughter," proclaimed the Earl, coming down the staircase.

She ran into his arms and embraced him.

"Father, oh, father. I am so glad to see you well again."

"And it warms my heart to have you home for Christmas, my dearest Moira," he sighed, tears welling up in his eyes.

A discreet cough drew Moira's attention to the fact that Stuart was standing patiently in the hall.

"Oh, Stuart, I am so sorry."

Moira took him by the arm and led him out of the shadows.

"Mother, father, you may remember Stuart Weston?"

"Heavens. Do forgive me, Mr. Weston, I had thought you to be one of the carriage staff," said the Countess, clearly flustered.

"No offence was taken, Lady Strathcarron," replied Stuart, bowing deeply.

"Mother, father, Stuart has asked me to marry him and with your permission, I intend to accept!"

Lord and Lady Strathcarron burst into chuckles of delight and the Earl shook Stuart warmly by the hand.

"We shall now retire to the library. Moira, Margaret, will you excuse us?"

He guided Stuart towards the library.

"Do you think father will say yes?" asked Moira, anxiously. "Stuart has just inherited the Brampton title and estates."

"Yes, we had heard the news and I am sure that your father will have no objections – he seems a fine young man. He attended the weekend we arranged when that awful Harwood was here, did he not?"

Moira nodded proudly.

"I have one question, mother. Why is there an Officer at the gates?"

"Harwood, it transpires, was part of a gang and the investigating Officers deemed it necessary to provide us with protection in case of repercussions. I cannot see that a gang would find their way here easily, but it makes us feel safer. There are men patrolling the grounds too."

Just then, Rankin entering with a telegram, interrupted the conversation.

"My Lady," he said, bowing.

"Ah, this will be from Ewen. No doubt he will have read the telegram that you missed. I expect he will be informing us of the time of his return to Lednock – "

The Countess ripped open the telegram, read it and cried aloud with joy.

"Mother, what is it?" asked Moira, wondering what else could now happen.

"Darling, it is yet more good news. It seems that we now have double the reason to celebrate. Ewen has proposed to a Miss Emily Tennant and she has accepted. Her father gave his consent this afternoon."

Moira and the Countess embraced.

At that very moment, the Earl and Stuart emerged from the library, beaming.

"Rankin. Bring up two bottles of champagne from the cellar. We are celebrating an engagement."

Stuart ran at once to Moira's side and took her hand.

"Darling, your father has consented – we can now plan our wedding."

"And that is not the only good news of the day. Ewen has proposed and been accepted, too. We shall be proud parents twice over," beamed the Countess.

After the popping of champagne corks, a toast was raised to the happy couples.

Stuart and Moira drank theirs, staring into each other's eyes, basking in their love.

*

Later beneath the stars, Moira and Stuart strolled to the very same vegetable garden where they had first met.

"Darling, look," he cried, pointing up to the sky, *"a shooting star*. Wish on it!"

Moira turned to Stuart, her heart so very full of love.

"What more could I wish for, my dearest? I have everything I could ever desire and more. I have a man I love more than the whole wide world, my family are safe and sound and now my brother is engaged to a darling girl. My love for you has brought us riches beyond compare."

Stuart pulled her closer, his eyes dark with emotion.

"In that case, how would you feel about a double wedding? We could send word to Ewen and set a date early in the New Year."

Moira gazed into Stuart's stunning blue eyes. This man she loved how fortunate she was that he was the most wonderful and the most caring man she had ever met.

"Oh, Stuart, that would make me the happiest woman alive, I could not ask for more."

His lips met hers in a kiss that told her everything she needed to know – for now, forever and for the rest of their lives spent in love together and on into eternity.

She could think of no greater happiness.

"My love," she murmured, "my own dearest love forever and ever."

32297284R00101

Printed in Poland
by Amazon Fulfillment
Poland Sp. z o.o., Wrocław